Praise for Stephen Graham Jones

"[Jones'] writing is hallucinogenic, varied, fascinating. While reading the novel, big names in writing came to mind: Pynchon, David Foster Wallace, even Faulkner." —*New Pages*

"The constant threat or fact of violence in [his] stories combined with Jones's idiosyncratic, staccato prose makes for gripping and visceral reading." —*Publishers Weekly*

"Imagine the laconic Sherman Alexie meeting the bombastic Stephen King on the Texas High Plains." —*Austin Chronicle*

"Jones' most powerful writing stems from his attempts to reconcile the two cultures by which he defines himself—or finds himself defined." —*Southwestern American Literature*

"For a while now I have felt that we Native American writers (and I most certainly include myself in the "we") keep writing about the same damn things. Stephen Graham Jones writes with a whole new aesthetic and moral sense. He doesn't sound like any of the rest of us, and I love that." —Sherman Alexie

"Painfully real and utterly hypnotic." —*Houston Chronicle*

"Jones' brisk, clean, visceral prose gives the novel its edgy suspense." —*Publishers Weekly*

Growing Up Dead in Texas

Also by Stephen Graham Jones

The Fast Red Road: A Plainsong
All the Beautiful Sinners
The Bird is Gone: A Manifesto
Bleed Into Me: A Book of Stories
Demon Theory
The Long Trial of Nolan Dugatti
Ledfeather
It Came From Del Rio
The Ones that Got Away
Seven Spanish Angels
Zombie Bake-Off

M P Publishing Limited
12 Strathallan Crescent
Douglas
Isle of Man
IM2 4NR
British Isles

A CPI Catalogue for this title is available from the British Library

This book is sold subject to the condition that it shall not, by way of trade or otherwise, be lent, resold, hired out, or otherwise circulated without the publisher's prior consent in any form of binding or cover other than that in which it is published and without a similar condition including this condition being imposed on the subsequent purchaser.

The scanning, uploading and distribution of this book via the internet or via any other means without the permission of the publisher is illegal and punishable by law. Please purchase only authorized electronic editions and do not participate in or encourage electronic piracy of copyrighted materials. Your support of the author's rights is appreciated.

Jones, Stephen Graham, 1972-
Growing up dead in Texas / by Stephen Graham Jones.
-- 1st ed.
p. cm.
ISBN-13: 978-1-84982-154-4
ISBN-10: 1-84982-154-2

1. Families--Texas--Fiction. 2. Small cities--Texas --Fiction. 3. Arson--Texas--Fiction. 4. Texas--Fiction. 5. Domestic fiction. 6. Detective and mystery stories. I. Title.

PS3560.O5395G77 2012   813'.6
QBI11-600228

All characters in this ~~photoplay~~ fiction are fictitious, and any resemblance to real persons, living or dead, is purely coincidental.

Cover design © Monica Gurevich/Julie Metz, Ltd.
Author photo by Gary Isaacs

"You should write all this down someday."

—B̲ETTY U̲NDERWOOD, to her daughter's boyfriend, when he was sixteen and never going to be a writer.

GROWING UP DEAD IN TEXAS

Stephen Graham Jones

MP PUBLISHING
WWW.MPPUBLISHINGUSA.COM

Preface

In the summer of 2008, I finally, and for good, I think, left West Texas. I'd tried a couple of times before—Florida, Arkansas—but the moves didn't take. Florida's sticky green was a nightmare to someone raised on dirt, someone scared of water, and Little Rock was what I'd been trained my whole life to hate: a city. Where I grew up, we didn't even have a post office. The church and the school were on the same grounds. Sometimes at recess the ball would go over the fence, into the graveyard, and then, walking stiff-legged through the headstones, you'd see the names of people who were sitting at your dinner table a year ago. What you do then is set your lips, focus ahead, and don't let yourself run for the fence, once you've got that ball again.

If you ever start running, I mean.

this, I'm smiling to be there again, yeah, is doing that hollow kind of pounding. across that fence. How guilty you while all these people are dead. I still Hot Wheels car nosed against the base by touch, and knowing it hadn't been neral. And how I wanted that car worse ouldn't even start to reach for it. Not in

And already, though I promised myself three paragraphs ago that there weren't going to be any lies this time, that this *wasn't* going to be a novel, still, I'm not telling you who's headstone that was, am I?

I don't know.

I probably shouldn't even be doing this—I've never written non-fiction. Not even sure I believe it's a possible thing, really. Sure, some of the stories I've had published, they're me as the main character, just with a different name, a cooler truck. And, yeah, the novels—each one's autobiography, never mind what kind of crazy stuff's going on. Fiction's always been my camouflage, the lie I hide behind, hoping nobody will recognize that that kid in the diner with his uncle, that kid wetting his pants from a grief so pure it scares him, makes him think he's dying too, that's me.

And now I'm in that diner again.

Fiction. I wish I were writing fiction this time. It's so much easier.

This, though, it's the only way I can go back, I think.

If I even should.

I

Chapter One

People in Greenwood, Texas remember where they were that morning.

This is before the news trucks came in from Midland and Odessa, even in from San Angelo and Lubbock, places you only ever went for a basketball tournament, or to shop for school clothes in August. It probably would have gone national for a blip or two—not that morning, but what would happen later—except there were fireworks in the sky that week, and nobody was looking anywhere but up.

This is where it starts, though.

North of Cloverdale and just east of the school, about a mile in from the Graham place but on the same side of the road. A series of three houses going back, if you count the tack shed the wind finally blew over a couple of weeks ago, nearly a hundred years. A porcupine's living in that tack shed now. There are no kids around anymore to chase it, to sneak in on their bellies, close their eyes and grab for a quill. Run away so fast that by the time they stop, their knees are stained green with cotton. The thin horseshoes are still there under the rotten boards, though, along with the buckles of saddles with stories nobody'll ever know. Nails lumped with rust but still solid.

An old yoke half chewed away by generations of puppies that should have known better than to ever grow into dogs. And spread all around for acres, so that they spill into the turnrows, old tractors and ramshackle plows, left where they broke, the husks of loyal trucks not for sale, faded beer cans on their dashboards, and trailers of every kind, their tongues hidden in last summer's careless weeds, some of those trailers mounded with farm sale steals that were never unloaded. Two barns, slat-board stables leaning closer and closer to the ground, and then the new blue-pipe arena, dirt still bermed up from where the regulation plastic barrels used to be. Five-hundred-gallon silver tanks on racks, for gas and farm-grade diesel—gravity hoses, not electric pumps—and a rut road wandering through it all, a horse trap ran along the side of the property with gates at either end, a chute on the house-side, a rickety windmill cocked against the sky, its concrete tank cracked open twenty years ago, all the moss dried and gone, the goldfish carried away by birds.

The King place, right about dawn.

Arthur King stands in the doorway for a moment before pointing his boot down to the porch, giving it what's left of his weight.

Out on Cloverdale a pumper flashes by, his truck chugging white smoke, his new tires singing on the asphalt.

Arthur King raises his cup to the pumper, groans down into his chair.

He still remembers when Cloverdale was 307. Hardly even that. A packed-dirt road that fell away sharp on both sides and went as far as you could see in either direction, connecting Midland with 137, which would crook you north into Stanton. Or, if you turned earlier, like everybody did back then, a cut-across to the gin.

Arthur King doesn't use the Stanton co-op anymore, though. Hardly anybody in Greenwood does.

It's not because of the low spot in the cut-across road where you can drag a low trailer if it's too long—though pulling six or seven daisy-chained cotton trailers up that hill's claimed a rear-end or two—it's that everybody remembers Earl Holbrook some, the guy who runs the Midland gin now. He did his last two years of high school at Greenwood, and put a lot of hours on a lot of tractors back when he was trying to make a go of it. Before he washed out, like nearly everybody else did a couple years back.

Everybody who was taking it just a year at a time, anyway.

Out on his porch that morning, Arthur King isn't smoking a cigarette to wake up, not anymore, but he can't seem to break the habit of stepping outside either. It's got to where he wonders if that was what it was all about in the first place, the smoking. He just wanted a few breaths to himself.

It's foolish. He smiles at it all, stands up just to lean down on the railing, spit a brown line down into his wife's flowerbed, survey the morning.

Inside, it's breakfast. Mrs. King is watching the news from the couch. The news is on, anyway.

Out here on the porch, it's just him, King. And his empire.

In every direction he looks, he's got land. Not all of it's his, but there's a section directly to the south, a half-section across the road from it to either side, and to the west, closer to the school, a half-section he still insists on running himself, won't lease out. Most of it irrigated, and more besides, patched together in a fifteen-mile spread.

At one time nearly all of it had been King land, but that was two generations back already. Inheritance has turned a continuous spread into a game of hopscotch, what with cousins selling their quarter-sections off, sometimes just ten acres at a time. King's bought what he can, sometimes secondhand even, at a mark-up, but still, more than he'd prefer's already in development. Everybody wants to live in tight little clusters of homes for some reason. Close enough to the school to see the stadium lights on Friday night, hear the drums rattle, the crowd swell with noise.

And there are the oil derricks, too, of course.

Even the cousins, hocking their land out for RVs and houses in town, have been smart enough to hang onto the mineral rights. Most of them, anyway. The ones who still make it to the reunion in the summer.

As for the rest, well.

Driving down Cloverdale, from Midland to Big Lake or wherever business or pleasure's taking them, they probably don't even know that either side of the ditch has their name on it, more or less.

The King land—in Greenwood, Texas in 1985—it's most of Greenwood. The Ledbetters still have a few patches, but ever since Old Man Marty died and there was no one to take the operation over, the fields are leased out, the Ledbetter girls, all but one of them with different names now, just waiting until the developers come knocking. The husbands they'd met at college in Abilene waiting too.

King's met all those husbands at one time or another—church, mostly, during the holidays—and has managed just to nod, shake their smooth hands, welcome them for the ten minutes they're investing in their future.

All they'll have's money, though.

Not land.

When Arthur King was still too young to really understand, his granddad had knelt down to one knee, nudged a toy tractor forward with the back of his index finger, and told

Little King—surely someone had to have called him that—that the trick with farming, it isn't so much being a good farmer, though that helps, yeah. The trick, the secret—he'd have had to whisper this part, his old-man breath smoky—it's farming your own land.

All boys being groomed to run a place, this is what they get told at one time or another.

It's what King told each of his four sons.

Two of them it scared off, into lives their great-grandfather never could have even guessed at, but for the one left alive, it finally stuck.

It's why King can have his coffee on the porch like this some mornings. Even early December mornings, when every other farmer in Midland county hasn't been home for two or three nights running.

If King had been out on the porch just before light, like usual (Mrs. King had been in the bathroom pawing at the tub faucets, and it had taken him a while to get her to understand that nobody had to get to school today), it would have looked like the Germans were invading. Lights shivering through thick dust, dust that shouldn't be raised like that in the nighttime.

You don't stop stripping cotton just because you lose the sun, though.

King remembers pulling thirty-hour shifts up in the seat, until the golden haze of his cab lights was the only thing that made any kind of sense, and his brain geared down to a kind of necessary stupidity, where all it knew anymore was how to line the headers up with the rows, how to tip the basket over into the buggy. How to start it all over again, and again, and again, listening for the brushes hard enough that their thrush seemed to come from his own chest, listening with enough of himself that he wouldn't have been a bit surprised to unsnap his shirt and see cotton churning in there.

Now, though, he has hands, good ones, dependable ones, and a son too, who knows the work anyway, even if it's just a fallback.

Not that King's letting go anytime soon, mind.

He nods to himself and clamps onto the porch railing, guides himself back into his chair.

Out there, blowing in, there's the cold dust the strippers are shaking up, and, under that, the oily tang of diesel, which, for reasons King's never understood, still makes his mouth water.

But there's something else this morning too.

King guides his coffee away from his face, to taste the air better. Cocks his head over like he can hear it, if he tries.

Finally, to be sure, he stands again, a jack-in-the-box of an old man, his coffee cup tumbling off the railing, finding a rock in the flowerbed, some old sandstone grinder his dad brought in forever ago, when they were everywhere, a nuisance.

King doesn't register the thick glass shattering. The steam holding to the grinder for a moment before letting go.

Instead he purses his lips, stares hard down the rows of naked reaching stalks spoked out from his house.

It can't be.

But he knows the smell too, has smelled it like this one time before.

"*Cecilia!*" he bellows from the porch, and she's inside on the couch, her hands curled in her lap, her posture a sparrow's posture, her small head turning all at once to this sound, this disturbance, this emergency.

What he wants is his hat, his keys, the goddamn phone.

The fields are on fire.

***

The last time Arthur King would have smelled cotton burning, in this quantity at least—small fires in the basket or the equipment aren't all that unusual—would have been 1963.

According to the Midland paper (Stanton's was only weekly then, and irregular at that), the Martin County co-op "became a sad conflagration of the season's already meager profits."

In short, sometime after the last cotton trailers had been parked in the lot west of the gin, one of the seasonal hands—in 1963, the trains still came through regularly—had supposedly ground out his cigarette as the manager insisted, warning them of the kind of tragedy that followed.

Though never questioned on the matter, as he never showed up to the gin again—guilty or not, there was no work, not even cleanup—what likely happened was that that hand, standing at the front corner of the gin, where he could be out of the north wind and still watch the cars slip past on the highway, ground his cigarette out then gathered himself to jog away from the building, latch onto the side rail of the truck that had just delivered the night crew, ride it to wherever a plate or a bed was for him.

Moments after he was gone, that cigarette remembered itself.

At first it would only be the dullest of orange glows, not even a spark, but in stripping season, especially around any gin, there's not a boot's space of packed dirt to be had. It's all cotton, stretched and blown into a dingy white pad.

It would only take that dull orange glow a moment to touch a strand of lint, and for that strand to pass the glow onto the next strand, and so on, until what happened happens.

The thing about cotton, too, is that it doesn't burn like paper or wood or anything normal. Instead it smolders, roiling off pungent black smoke, like a stack of tires, the orange worms crawling there just under the black, but you can never step on them all. Stepping on them only gives the smolder more air, and water only flares it up for a few moments.

All of which is to say that cotton, it only stops burning when the cotton's gone.

In 1963, King would have been nearly forty, working some of the outlying dryland fields for his father until he somehow got them to produce, could graduate to one of the two fields with a shiny new Tri-Matic lined up along the fence, and Mexicans to help roll it out.

King would have undoubtedly been one of the men who came not to try to douse the cotton—though the grainy photographs do show an old Diamond T fire truck there, from Lenorah when it was a town—but to simply stand and watch.

It was the worst thing anybody had ever seen. The following morning, the men, whose trailers were so covered in soot that they would have to scrape the black off to find their stenciled- or welded-on names, they didn't come directly home. They walked through their stripped fields instead, the skin of their faces still drawn tight from the heat. They wouldn't be drilling their fingers into the soil for moisture, or searching for lost tools or arrowheads, but probably finding the boll or two still out there, still clinging to the odd stalk. Finding those leftover bolls and then walking past them, their lips held tight, their eyes set on next season, if the bank would only understand about this season.

But that's always the story.

***

Arthur King wasn't the only one to smell the fire that morning, though.

On December 4th, 1985, Cloverdale became a parking lot. Trucks slowed to a stop one after the other, the drivers standing in the ditch on the south side of the road, their hats worked back off their foreheads so they could squint better. And after the trucks, all the station wagons coming back from dropping the kids off, the mothers inside just sitting behind the wheel, whispering to themselves about Christmas. What they were going to do now, this time.

The smell even made it all the way to school that morning, so that Mr. Brenhemin, the shop teacher, cocked his welding helmet up—he always made you use the torch outside, even if there was still frost on everything, because he never trusted anybody to tell between regular steel and galvanized—held his gloved hand out to the side, for quiet.

And then the class caught the scent, followed it around the edge of the building.

A half mile off, straight across the field to the east, there was the smoke.

Nobody said anything.

***

An hour before that, give or take, Belinda King, Arthur King's daughter-in-law, wife to his son who finally stayed, is standing in her kitchen, staring out the screen door like every morning. Waiting for the day to start. Just one more cup of coffee.

What she really needs to be doing, she knows, is cleaning Thanksgiving out of the refrigerator. But then she really needs to be doing a lot of things, she supposes.

Right now, anyway, she's just staring.

Her husband Rob's out there somewhere, running a buggy maybe, because the high school kid (Tommy Moore, a senior) didn't show again, or maybe teaching one of the hands how to build a module so it doesn't fall apart, or maybe just working the pedals of a stripper, trying not to drag any guide wires down this year, for once.

Belinda smiles, covers it with her hand.

What she remembers of stripping is her dad letting her and her brothers ride back in the basket. How they would scream and squeal whenever one of the two headers—strippers were small in the late sixties, in Lamesa—sucked up a rat, spit it down onto them, so that they'd be trapped with it until they could get their dad's attention. How he'd always pretend not to understand what the problem was, almost until they were crying with what she'd later understand was joy.

Right beside the screen door she's holding open now is the dryer, three pairs of pants tumbling in it. Just behind that, on the way through the kitchen into the living room, three boys in their underwear, eating cereal.

The pants weren't wet when she woke up, but they were cold. Not as warm as her boys needed, anyway.

If Rob were here, he'd stand at the sink, looking out the window at the day, raise his coffee cup to his mouth then lower it deliberately, ask her why his sons have to sit around the kitchen table half-dressed like that. What if somebody comes to the door for him? Staring out the window the whole time, as far away as he can.

Belinda's best mental snapshot is of him doing just that a few mornings ago.

It's her worst, too.

What she tells herself is that he's right, probably. That maybe boys shouldn't sit around in their underwear for breakfast. It's not proper. No way to start the day.

This morning, though, it's just her and them. So.

What Belinda tells herself is that she knew what she was getting into, marrying a farmer. That this is better than the early days anyway, when Rob had the side-row on a four-hour cycle so that he was easing that spindly chain along twice a night. Coming back to bed shaking from cold. Sleeping in his boots. Backing his truck out before he'd really even woke up again.

It had been stupid and wonderful, and she wouldn't trade it for anything.

That had been in the old house, though, the small one at the King Place. The one the main hand Miguel lives in now.

This one, it's one of five, built in a wagon circle around a cul-de-sac cut ten acres deep into a field never taken out of CRP, so that, instead of cotton, what she looks out onto is a half-section of tufted yellow grass in every direction. Maybe what the county looked like before the Spanish cattle brought the mesquite in.

All along the brick half-wall around the flowerbed in front are the rocks and grinders and rusted-solid tools the boys have found out in the fields. For most of the summer there'd been a series of eight cloudy old telegraph or telephone insulators, the kind made of glass that you can still find buried in a line in some pastures if you're willing to walk. But ever since Jonas, her oldest, got that new .22, they went the way of every other bottle she hadn't thought to lock away.

It's just as well. It's better he broke them up out in the grass than them blowing off their perch, shattering on the welcome mat. And they would have two weeks ago, when the wind came like she couldn't remember, like it had forgot it was November. It made Belinda miss their old house on the King Place. There, they'd always had the horses to watch. If Macaroni or Tall Boy started rolling their eyes and blowing, rearing up to pull the slats of the corral down, then Rob would herd her and the boys out to the old cellar. He'd lean back on the drill-bit counterweight so that only his boot heels were touching dirt and they'd feel their way down the crumbly rock stairs, hide until the clouds had drawn their funnels back up into the sky.

Underground like that, even counting the time the bullsnake had climbed the wall to try to hiss them out of its den, she'd felt safe. So what if the house blew away, if the tractors all got piled up on the other side of the property?

In the cellar, she had what was important.

This new house, though, it was all above the ground.

After the wind—Rob had been sandfighting the insurance dryland like everybody else, the blowing sand scraping electricity up from the ground so that the poles all around his field were lighting up like candles, telling him to get his plow out of the ground—after the windows stopped shaking, Belinda lifted the mattress off the bathtub, let the boys climb out, two of them crying.

They were all right, though. Safe.

It had just been wind, not a tornado. Not this late in the season. But: "Mom."

It was Jonas, at the sink window.

He was so grown-up.

Belinda went to the sliding glass door, looked out.

Their trampoline, it was tangled in the fence across the pasture, its black skin hanging slack now, flapping slow, trash from the burn barrels still fifty feet in the air, in no hurry to settle. And the drums Rob had lined up by the shop were all toppled, seeping Paraquat down so that nothing was going to grow there for ten years. And their pump house, the one Rob and Jonas had built together while the roofing crew was nailing shingles down on the house, it had simply exploded.

Belinda smiled just to keep from going the other way, then sucked her lower lip in. Pulled her boys close so they could see too, understand: this is where you live.

"Let's pray for your father now," she said, and closed her eyes.

***

Greenwood, Texas. 1985.

According to the old plaque in front of the church, the name comes from the Reverends Green and Wood, who came to West Texas for what must have been some good reason, I guess. It doesn't matter. What happened—it's easy to tell—is that they planted a church, and a community grew up around it.

That's the boring way to say Greenwood, though.

There's a better way.

Toilets.

In 1978, we moved to Midland for two years, to make a go of it in town. No real clue why, and it's too late to ask. Before that we'd been living pretty much with grandparents, though there's a picture I found once, of a square little whitewashed house I have no memory of. It's just sitting out in the middle of nowhere. I'm on the porch in a striped shirt, my feet apart, knees knocked together.

It's gone now, of course, that picture. One of the old ones that were rough like fabric on the front but somehow smooth too, like the picture was wet, or silk. There used to be home movies, too, but they're all gone as well.

I'm thinking that's why I'm trying to write it all down, maybe.

I have to have come from somewhere, I mean.

But the toilets.

When we moved to Roosevelt Street in Midland, Texas, my clearest memory is of standing in the bathroom and flushing the toilet over and over and over. There was enough water pressure for that. All I'd ever known before, the way I thought it was, was that you flushed a toilet once and then you waited a long time for the tank to fill and usually just got tired of waiting, went and did something else.

Town was magic, though.

I pushed that handle until I got in trouble, and then kept pushing it every chance I got, the best secret ever, like how I'd sometimes see the moon pale in the sky during daytime, and know that I was the only one who could.

But we came back, of course. To Greenwood. In houses and trailers all over the district, with well water and septic tanks, no water pressure to speak of.

And please understand here, that name, "King," it's not what I mean.

Or, it's exactly what I mean.

And I say that the toilets are the thing I remember best about Roosevelt Street, but there's something else too.

In second grade, my last year there, my mom woke me up one night.

I was in the kitchen, at the back door. A butter knife in my hand, wedged in between the strike plate and the tongue.

I have no idea what I was trying to do, but not long after that we moved back. It's the only time I've ever sleepwalked.

***

As for Rob King that morning the cotton burned, he'd been awake then for nearly forty hours straight.

There were more to come, too.

He doesn't die in some heroic way here either, using a neighbor's backhoe to try to scrape dirt up around the fire, control it. He isn't the one in that graveyard, I mean.

By the time he caught scent of the fire, probably thirty minutes before his dad did, on the other side of Cloverdale, it's estimated to have been already burning for at least eight hours.

That's the way it is with cotton.

That hand at the Stanton co-op who ground his cigarette out under his boot could have been on his way to breakfast, not dinner.

What cotton does is draw the heat in, let it grow, let it send its hot tendrils out, and by the time it surfaces, it's hours and hours too late. All over the world, riverside warehouses have burned because one cotton bale was delivered two days ago with a secret ember for a heart.

By the time Rob King knew his crop was on fire, it was too late.

And it wasn't what you might be picturing, either: knee-high flames moving fast and nearly invisible across a field, leaving only ashes in their wake.

A field in CRP, or hay grazer, it'd go like that, sure. Fast, so all you could do is get out of the way, try to drive ahead of it, open the gates for whoever's cattle are in the next pasture. That happens all the time, from all the usual suspects—cigarettes, lightning, downed power lines, bottle rockets, truck exhausts. Even just cutting the metal ties from under a trailer home before you move it, those red-hot ends can start a grass fire.

A cotton field in December won't go like that, though.

The plants are dead, definitely, you couldn't strip any other way, but the chemicals the planes have already dusted them with to open the bolls and kill the plant, they've left an oily residue that you can smell on somebody's pants when they finally come home, and those chemicals, for some reason they don't burn.

No, the only way to lose your year's crop to fire, at least in the field, it's at the end of stripping season, when your cotton's sitting at the edge of all the fields in blocky, rectangular modules, waiting for the trucks to come for them.

Before module builders—picture a camper big enough to live in, but made of thick metal, with Death Star walls that press the cotton you dump in into a tight, dense block, and, when you're a kid, not old enough to drive a stripper yet, this is where you always end up, which is right where you want to be: the handles of the module builder in your too-big gloves, thousands upon thousands of pounds of pressure at your fingertips now, the best video game ever—before module builders, farmers had to deliver their cotton to the gin in rickety trailers, but you lose a lot that way. Both cotton and time.

With modules, all you do after you've made one is hook onto the builder and pull it a couple of lengths forward, holding your breath each time, because if you've done it even a little bit wrong, the modules can calve off five-hundred-pound sheets of themselves.

After that, all you do is sling a fitted tarp over the top, call the gin for a number to spray paint onto each end, and only worry if the rain comes before the truck does. And the ditches of all the roads that lead to the gin, they're not white like snow anymore for Christmas, but Christmas is going to be better for that.

The trucks that pick the modules up, too, they're kind of amazing. They angle their flat beds back to get a lip under the cotton, and then the wide belt on the floor groans into motion, pulling the whole module up, in. If that was all there was, though, the modules would fall apart—they weigh too much to be dragged like that. So, the fix is to gear the truck's rear end with those rollers, and synch them up, so that as it pulls the module up and in, it's also backing under it. What it looks like more than anything is a snake swallowing an egg: a slow process you can hardly look away from. It makes you realize how small you are.

Ask any kid in Future Farmers of America why he wants to be a farmer, and he won't have that solid an answer: it's honest work, you're your own boss; "it's all I know." Mine—

Greenwood Independent School District's always had a strict hair code—was that I could have my hair as long as I wanted, and never have to tuck my shirt in again.

All those reasons are lies, though.

None of us were ever articulate enough to get at what it really was. We could feel it, sure, but would never admit something like that.

Watching a module builder pack fifteen bales' worth of cotton into one thick block, or taking a double-fold disk to a field in March, so that by the end of the day you've covered hundreds of acres, had fourteen hawks following your each turn, for the mice and rabbits you scare up, it's a connection. You to something bigger. Out there in the kind of quiet left after ten hours of your tractor grinding, you're part of it all, and don't have to say anything about it, can just, for a moment, be.

You know you'll never be rich, but that's only if you measure wealth by money. That old saying, yeah. Sew it on a pillow if you want.

Ask how I got here, anyway, behind a keyboard instead of out in the field, and I'll say that this wasn't my first choice. Really, it's a complete betrayal of who I used to be.

I didn't go to college to get a career, I went to college because I thought Lubbock, Texas would be cool. They got more concerts than the Ector County Coliseum. Even when I graduated, my plan was to come home, lease a tractor, custom farm for ten years or so, and read books alone in my trailer the nights I wasn't in town, looking for the girl from TG Sheppard's "Slow Burn," that dark hair falling cross her shoulders, *being* that guy trying to find his way home in Roseanne Cash's "Seven Year Ache."

Even that morning of the fire, though, I think I already knew I wasn't staying, that I was running away the first chance I got.

And I still haven't told you about Rob King.

***

Pete Manson knows better than I do, really.

I never worked directly for him in high school, though I did help arrange toolbars and trailers when he went under a few years later, was having to get things lined up for the auction. The whole time he just stood by the barn and smoked cigarette after cigarette. I had no idea what to say to him, and knew that if I even tried, we'd end up where we always did: his nubbed ring finger.

Back when he was in high school, he'd vaulted down from the mounded top of a cotton trailer, caught his graduation ring on a stray wire so that his finger stayed up there.

Because of him, I never wore any rings or watches when I was working. So maybe I owe my hands to him, I don't know.

But, Pete.

He was from my mom's generation, but from Stanton, not Lamesa. Back then, they all seemed to know each other somehow. I've never understood it completely, especially since, when I was coming up, you didn't go to Stanton alone if you didn't want to get jumped.

Whenever she talks about him, though, she's talking about his younger brother, the one who died. It was Halloween, and my mom and Pete and the rest of whoever was there (I never asked) were in the back of a pick-up, out in some field. Pete's little brother had tagged along, but promised not to say anything about the beer.

I'm guessing on that part, but that's just because my mom cleans all her stories up.

Anyway, they were out there just tooling around, and Pete's little brother kind of fell out the back, like happens all the time.

He held on to the bed rail for a bit but then lost it, probably kicked free enough to not get clipped by the bumper.

Everybody yelled and laughed for the truck to stop, and Pete's little brother was okay, of course—it had only been two or three feet down, after all, and they weren't pulling a trailer—so somebody raised their hand to guide the driver back, pick the kid up.

Except Pete's little brother didn't get up when he should have. Maybe he'd had the wind knocked out of him? Maybe he was embarrassed?

I have to imagine he was looking the other way, anyway.

Slowly, with Pete watching, with all of them watching, none of them able to get the driver's attention, the truck's rear wheel backed over Pete's little brother's head.

That's where the story always ends, too. With Pete looking down at his little brother. Taking that image with him.

I never asked for more, for the accusations that must have been everywhere, the weeks and months of screaming. All the people at church all the time.

The only way I even know, or think I know, it was Halloween, it's that my mom, once when she was driving me to the doctor and telling it, about to cry again, she said how Pete's little brother's head, it had been like a pumpkin.

He wasn't the only dead kid I grew up with, though.

There was also somebody else's brother, brained when the rim popped up from a tire he was working on. There was another kid, diving down into the stock tank of a windmill, the lip of an old barrel waiting for him just under the surface. My best friend's brother shot in the face, on accident, with a shotgun, or another friend racing a train, almost making it. And more and more and more, so that by the time you make it to fifteen, you feel charmed, bulletproof. Able to live up to all of the stories your uncles probably shouldn't have told you. Able to, one night, driving home the long way from a dance in Odessa, the fog thick, turn your headlights off and bury the pedal, trust that Telephone Pole Road's just going to keep being there, mile after mile. Or that if it's not, then you probably deserve that too.

But, Pete.

When I go see him now, he's back in the game, farming. Everybody who washes out, they come back again. And he's not a small man, either. Six feet up and four around, the way he says it, his right eye glinting. Still smoking every chance he gets. Big enough that he's taken to wearing bib overalls, now. Carhartt brown but faded to the color of blown sand, the brim of his hat curled in on itself the way we used to all try to do in elementary.

Flying Southwest, he has to purchase two seats.

But it doesn't matter: the seats are comp, courtesy of The Mirage. Las Vegas.

What Pete Manson learned from the first time he washed out was that it was all a game, all a gamble. Flying to Nevada every other weekend to work the tables for two- and three-day stretches, it's the same thing, more or less. He's making it work, anyway, though he won't tell me what his game is, or his strategy. Maybe he still remembers me lining up his cotton trailers for the bank, I don't know.

I catch him on a Friday, on his way to the Midland International Airport, and have to ride all the way there with him if I want to talk, leave my truck at his place.

"Mind?" he says, flashing a cigarette between us, then rolls my window down before I can answer.

On his dashboard are the rags and wrenches and pamphlets and papers you have to leave on your dash if you want to keep it from cracking open in the sun. I hold one of the crackly pages of something down for him; usually it's just his window blowing.

"So you want to know about Tommy Moore?" he says, cranking the wheel west.

I shrug sure, like it's his idea. Like Tommy Moore's not exactly what I had my uncle prime him with on the phone.

Pete hisses a laugh out, blows smoke into the cab.

He never had any kids. One wife, but she left with the first farm—with one of the other farmers there to buy equipment for pennies on the dollar. Pete can wear bib overalls every day of the week if he wants to now, I mean. The same pair, even.

He laughs again, thinking about it all, I guess, and my eyes are wet from the smoke but I don't want him to know that.

And, Tommy Moore.

I've only ever seen him once, when I was sixteen. At a bar in Midland, the second Rumors. I'd got in all the usual ways. But Tommy Moore. One of the kids from my grade, Shane, he'd always had a half-moon dented in under his eye. It was from playing in the burn barrels, poking the fire with a stick until an aerosol can exploded up into his face. Another friend, Scott, had melted-looking skin all on his temple, from being dragged around by a dog when he was still in diapers.

Tommy Moore was worse than both of them put together.

He'd seen me looking too, had held my eyes over his beer for a few seconds too long.

I lowered my hat, hid in the bathroom for the next few songs, sure he was coming in after me. That I was going to apologize if he did.

He must have been about twenty, then. Twenty-one, maybe. His face the same as it had been since his senior year. Like it always would be.

Now, riding in the truck with Pete Manson, who was there that morning in 1985, I have no idea where Tommy Moore might be.

That's a real name, too. It feels wrong to make everything okay by changing it.

The rest of this isn't exactly what Pete Manson says to me, though.

Close enough, I hope.

"Robert had been up then for about three days, I guess, shit. You know how it is, right, boss?"

His hand, clapping onto my knee.

And, *boss*. Because I've been to school. Because I don't have to drive a tractor.

"Tommy was in school then," I say.

"Should have been, yeah," Pete says. "But not that morning."

By now we're past 1120, past 1140, all the way to the sewage treatment plant—the "stinky bridge," growing up—almost to Midland, where Cloverdale becomes Florida if you don't hook it north up Fairgrounds.

I hold my breath against the smell, am probably remembering it more than really tasting it on the air, and Pete smiles, shrugs his huge shoulders, says, "Why you even want to know?"

"You were there."

He eyeballs me, shifts to the rearview mirror. Comes back to the road in front of us.

"Tommy wasn't bad, really," he tells me. "You know how it is being seventeen, stupid as a jackrabbit and twice as horny."

"He didn't deserve it, you mean."

Pete blows smoke, smiles behind it.

"Still don't know why you're asking, amigo."

"I just want to know."

"Said the spider to the…what is it?"

"What?"

"No, it's 'said the snake to the—the—' Nothing. Screw it."

I suddenly want to ask him about his little brother. Just what his name was, even. If he remembers my mom like she used to be. What she did after that day. What all of them did.

His answer, probably: "Still doing it, kid."

I never should have got in the truck with him.

"You were *there*," I tell him.

He looks across at me, no smile now. Finally nods, tongues his lip out.

"Okay then. What the hell. Sheryl Ledbetter?"

Blank stare from me.

"Ms. Godfrey?" he adds, his voice higher, mocking.

Ms. Godfrey. *Sheryl* Godfrey. Senior English, more than twenty years ago.

Pete nods, accelerates through the yellow light at Illinois, glaring into his mirror for blue and red lights.

"Bet you didn't know that part, did you?" he says, firing up another cigarette. "Nobody does, hoss."

He holds the pack out to me but I just say it back to him: "Ms. Godfrey?"

Pete studies his cigarette like the story's all right there. Like he's reading it from that thin white paper.

"Her and Tommy." He shrugs. "She'd come to see him on the way to school, then he kind of, you know, convinced her to stay, yeah?"

Ms. Godfrey. Seventeen years old, walking through a half-stripped field to bring breakfast to Tommy Moore.

Or something.

This would have been a thrill, twenty years ago.

Now, now it's like something being stolen from me.

I lick my lips, nod that I get it, yeah.

"And you don't want any of that kind of action in the cab of 4440 now, do you?" He laughs. "If you have a choice, I mean."

"The modules," I hear myself saying.

It's the part I never heard. The part only the people who were there know, I guess. And never told.

Pete eases onto 20 proper, and for a few hundred yards we pace a plane coming in to land.

He shrugs, says, "Then you know it all, then. They were up there fooling around. It could have just as easy been me, I mean. Any of us."

He's right, too.

In West Texas, there's no trees, no contour to the land.

If you want to hide, if you want a little privacy, all you can do, really, is climb up onto something. And, if you're helping a girl up behind you, then the stretched-tight tarp of a packed module's a lot better mattress than a pumpjack or water tank.

Which is where Rob King found them.

Unlike every other farmer in the county, in the history of farming maybe, none of Rob King's trucks ever had glasspacks. You don't put loud pipes on your truck because you think you're still in high school, either, but because, after driving a tractor all day, getting in a truck so quiet you can't hear it run, it's creepy, makes you feel like a ghost, and you can pop your timing chain, turning the key over when the truck's already started.

Maybe because he always insisted on sticks, though, had an aftermarket RPM bolted onto the dash—I honestly don't know, never thought to ask—Rob King had a truck that could sneak up on somebody like that.

He wasn't even looking for them, was just following his nose. That's the thing that probably still tears Tommy Moore up, if he thinks about it. But he's got to.

The module they were bedded down on top of, it was on fire. Slow fire, deep inside. Which Tommy Moore would have known ten minutes earlier if he'd have been thinking half-straight.

He had a Ledbetter girl up there, though, was a long way from any kind of rational thought.

Even when she was leading us through Hal Borland or "The Stone Boy" or prepositions, I mean, Ms. Godfrey, you could definitely have ideas you didn't plan on.

And what I'd guess is that Rob King, at first he figured that Tommy Moore'd already split for school, had left the stripper idling like that because he'd seen Rob's truck coming, figured it was his shift. The black cotton Rob was smelling, he figured it was coming from the basket, was still contained.

But then there's a naked arm suddenly over the blue edge of the tarp, and then a face, and—this is where things go wrong—that face, it's Tommy's, and clamped in his lips is a cigarette, the cherry so red, so wrong, Tommy Moore's eyes thin and satisfied at first.

After that, it's all legend.

Rob King dragging Tommy Moore down, beating him long after what little fight there was was over, and nobody pulling him off until Pete Manson and Arthur King got there in the same truck.

By that time it was too late, though.

Tommy Moore wasn't getting up on his own for a couple of weeks yet.

According to Pete Manson, Arthur King planted his hand on Pete's shoulder that day, so his old man legs wouldn't fail. And Pete was proud to be solid enough to hold onto.

Out in the field before them now, the deputies are chasing Rob King down, all three of them falling again and again, Rob

King's right hand cut deep across the knuckles, one of his boots coming off.

He's running for the buggy, and the tractor tied to it.

Pete laughs at how stupid it all was. That, then, none of them even knew that it wasn't just that one module burning up, it was twenty-five modules, for a mile all around. An act of arson Tommy Moore paid for with his face, paid for with the rest of his life. An act nobody ever quite figured out, especially with what happened later.

But they all quit trying, too.

They didn't *have* to make it make sense.

"Well," Pete says, collecting his duffel from the bed of the truck.

I pat the bed of his truck in farewell, cringe from a plane blasting off just over our heads, and like that he's walking away, turning sideways to fit between two cars.

For a few minutes I move a bent prybar back and forth in the bed of his truck, try to imagine what it was in its first life—tie rod from one of the tricycle tractors?—then swallow, turn back to the east, Greenwood thirty miles away now, and realize I don't even know anybody's number out there anymore.

Chapter Two

That night we all wanted the belly of the clouds to glow red like they did when a pasture was burning.

But of course cotton's not like that.

Instead, like Pearl Harbor Day was suddenly a big deal in West Texas—all the veterans I knew back then were Air Force or Army, not Navy—everybody put their flags out on their porches, not just Arthur King, like usual.

Tommy Moore's legendary big brother was enlisted, out there somewhere, so maybe it was all for him. To call him back.

There was a prayer meeting, of course, for Tommy. Everybody knew by then that it hadn't been him.

Arthur King climbed into his truck, directed it to Midland, to see if he still knew the Sheriff enough to come back with Rob.

He didn't.

Outside, all around the school, all over Greenwood, it was just butane pumps popping in the night. There was talk of canceling the make-up football game on Friday, even, but it was Stanton, the Buffaloes, so we couldn't cancel. There were more fights than usual in the parking lot, though, and the band at halftime broke formation when two of the trombone players looked up into the stands and started crying.

Their mothers came out onto the field, led them to the red clay track, walked around it with them until they were out of the light.

The ribbons that week were SHOOT THE BUFFS, same as every year. I held hands with a girl in the stands for the first time ever, even though she was already moving away.

I don't know what else to say about it, really.

How about this: way back in fourth grade, Ms. Easton's history—one of three teachers who ever believed in me—we'd all had to read reports on some local event. We either had to look it up in the library, get it from the papers, or interview somebody.

Kelly Janer interviewed her aunt, who told the story of being a girl up in Tulia, how they had an old cellar for when the tornadoes came.

Not if the tornadoes came, but when.

The story that Kelly told was about how her aunt, when she was our age, remembers her dad building her just-married sister a house right next door to their house. The cellar, it was between the two houses. It made sense. So—Kelly's mom had written this like always, we could all tell from the way Kelly was reading it, her lips all proper, in imitation—one day when the clouds were trailing what looked like smoke at their southeast edges, the sky green and quiet like it can get, everybody from both houses ran for the cellar. Only, at the metal door, there was this awkward moment, this bad piece of luck.

Kelly's aunt's big sister, she was pregnant at the time, and pretty far along.

And Kelly's aunt, that month she had measles.

They couldn't both go down into that cellar.

So what happened, Kelly said, why her aunt chases tornadoes now and is probably going to die from it someday, is that she had to stand out there by the door, holding onto the cable so tight that the rusted cable left a print in her jaw, her family all right there under her until the storm passed.

I always wanted to have a dream about that, about being that girl left up there like that for the storm, my hair lifting all around me, but you don't get to choose, I guess.

Me, I went for the library option, looked up the Stanton co-op fire in my grandmother's scrapbook, recited what I could. Nobody cared, least of all me.

Michael Graham got a few laughs, though. What he'd done at the last minute was make a two-page list. The title was "Things The Wind Has Taken Away." What he had listed were frito pies and hats and homework, especially—grinning at us over the top of his paper—*homework*.

Ms. Easton looked over her glasses at him, about this. Tried not to smile, I think.

We all wished we'd thought of that list, too. All had one ready, I mean, and were calling it out to him.

It was a hard act for Adam Moore to follow. Tommy's littlest brother.

Because even as a freshman Tommy had already been a basketball star, Adam got his report from the box of newspapers his dad had saved. It was a run-through of last year's district-winning season, of all the juniors returning that year as seniors, and then he broke down each player's stats, finally trailed off when none of us were listening. Making a show of not listening, really. If we could have made cricket sounds with our mouths, we would have.

"Good, good," Ms. Easton said, and then the bell rang and we were gone, and I never thought about that Stanton fire again until about a month ago, I don't think.

Kelly Janer's aunt's story, though, it made sense just a year or two later, when I got to know her better, doing homework at her house, back in her bedroom, the door always open, her mom never more than a few feet down the hall. Her mom who had obviously written that report for her. Her mom who was that older sister, who had got to step down into that cellar. Kelly the oldest of her daughters, the first one, the one who had to be protected from the measles, from bad grades, from boys—from me.

If not for her aunt, though, then Kelly, right? Who wouldn't even be at the front of the class to read that story then.

And, Adam. Adam Moore.

He won all-tournament in Crane as a sophomore, all-state his senior year, when basketball made regionals, but he fought too much in the parking lots too. He's a roofer in Odessa now, in spite of his picture-book jumper, the way he could just launch back and hold, hold, release. The last I heard of him, I was already at college. He was doing the Midland thing. What it involved, mostly, was fighting, at least until he met a certain Stanton Buffalo in a field just north of town, one of the ones being converted to a neighborhood, so that it still had volunteer cotton coming up around the poles.

Did he remember that Stanton's who we played that first Friday, after the fire?

I think so, yeah.

It's the first thing I thought when I heard about it, anyway.

As to who that Buffalo was, it doesn't matter. Or, I don't want to make up a name for him. It's enough that he came from a family known for fighting, and took Adam down fast and easy.

But Adam, he wouldn't stay down. That was always the thing about him.

He came back again and again, and each time that Buffalo put him down, a little harder each time, until it got to where he had Adam flat against the ground, had a scrap piece of concrete held up above his head, above *both* their heads, screaming to Adam that all he had to do was say Stop and it could be over. That that was all he had to do.

    Adam was Adam, though.

    He's still fighting, I know.

* * *

As for that report I'd done two years before all this, it gave me zero insight into the fire. It was just a stupid report, I mean.

    Peeling back through the microfiche now, though—we all should have been reading those old papers.

    Three weeks to the day after the Stanton gin burned to the ground, an unidentified man was found dead just past the Martin County line, over into Glasscock. It wouldn't have even made the Stanton paper except it was a couple of Stanton kids who'd followed the black funnel of birds out into the mesquite.

    It was 1963, sure, but still, it was obvious the man hadn't died from natural causes. Unless pipes and ropes can count as natural.

    And I don't even want to go back, put faces on the men behind the headlights whatever night that happened.

    I do know that, once, sent to get a part from an old neighbor I only knew to nod to, when he didn't answer the door, I did what you always do: went around to the shop.

    It was one of those sun-bleached ones, patched over with sheets of corrugated tin, just waiting to fall down.

    I could tell that he only worked in the front part of it anymore, the high wooden bench with the grinder and the vise and the red and green loops of his torch. Back in the cobweb darkness, it was the usual leftover tractors and baskets from a farm winding down, forgetting itself. Not antiques, just trash.

This place, too, this neighbor, he was just back from the cut-across road to Stanton. Meaning he would have been using the Stanton gin that season. Would have had his cotton checked in there, before the fire.

I called his name out, got nothing back, and was about gone when a dull flash back in the junk part of the shop stopped me. A thousand coincidences of light and dust and angle had to line up for me to see it, and even then it was just some whiteness. A dab of reflection there in the grime.

I looked behind me, for a shadow filling the door, but I was alone.

I shrugged one shoulder for nerve, walked across that concrete floor, and got close enough to the white to see what had reached out for me: an old but still sturdy chair, wood, with a back that didn't go up very high, like a barstool. But where it stopped, there was a flat curved panel, I guess you'd call it. A flat enough place to write something on with paint so thick that the wood had dried out under it, leaving the letters raised.

KKK.

I looked immediately up to a row of old tires stacked side by side on a shelf. So I could say that's what I'd been looking at.

But I was still the only one there.

I walked out nodding to myself, lost in the complicated switchbacks of some fake thought, and only when I looked back did I see what I'd left: footprints in the dust, going all the way back. To no other place but that chair.

I didn't get whatever part I'd come back for, and sitting behind my steering wheel, my thumb cocked around the ignition, I understood for the first time why Rob King had never wanted loud pipes on his truck.

***

Rob King. Robert Allen King.

His initials don't spell anything.

And Arthur King didn't have enough pull anymore to spring him from Midland lockup, but Rob King's face never showed up in the *Midland Reporter-Telegram* either.

Maybe it wasn't news to Midland people, though. 1985 was a lull between oil booms. The early eighties had been extravagant, everybody driving off at any time of the day for their cabins in Ruidoso, to bet on the dogs, shoot at the fish, buy some knee-high moccasins, and by the late eighties everybody would have tanning beds in their bedrooms, phones in their trucks, the phones tied into their horns and headlights so that at any of the Mexican food joints on the east side of town, the parking lots would jangle and flash all through lunch.

Farmers beating each other up out in the fields had nothing to do with the price of a barrel of oil, I mean, so, no, Rob King was booked with no fanfare, was released two days later to no protest.

On the way back, though, cutting across 1120, which was mostly still just trailers and roughed-in houses, Arthur King took his foot off the accelerator.

Another truck was parked in the ditch, on their side of the road, the chrome backs of its side mirrors winking in the sun.

Mr. Moore.

"No, stop," Rob King said to his dad, when Arthur King was pretending not to know who was waiting for them. For Rob King.

Arthur King thinned his old-man lips and pulled over a good ten yards past Moore.

They didn't say anything across the cab to each other, father to son. King didn't even look across, was just watching Moore in the side mirror. Watching his son walk into that reflection, one of his hands still trailing gauze.

Rob King didn't have to say he was sorry. Or, the way he said it was by staring straight at Moore the whole way, holding his eyes, not letting them go.

Moore probably rubbed a stray grain of dip from his mouth, then, once Rob King was close enough, he took him down with the tire beater he'd had run down alongside his right leg. Just like he'd been promising himself to.

And then he flipped the tire beater into the tall grass of the ditch so this wouldn't get out of hand and followed Rob down to the pavement, until Rob had to cover his face with arms.

At some point Mr. Moore's watch slung loose, hung in the air, clattered down. And the asphalt was probably hot enough that Rob's back left a slight, temporary depression in it, one that would have held a drink or two of water that night if it had rained.

But he never fought back, Rob King.

Both of them crying in their way, there in the daylight. Both of them small and furious and sad in Arthur King's side mirror.

Finally Arthur King stepped down from the truck, his shoulders heavy, his cheeks slack, his twelve-gauge bellowing once up into the sky, and that's how I want to leave them for now.

***

By this time, two days, forty-eight hours later, last night's victory over the Buffaloes hollow, a different story of the fire was surfacing. Not from the Sheriff's office either. Not to say anything bad about them, but they never matched anyone to those twenty-five burnt-down modules, never found that smoking match. But then they could only see it from the outside.

They had to have heard the stories, though.

Two of the deputies back then even had connections to Greenwood—one had gone there for two years of high school, before transferring to Robert E. Lee in town, and the other was married to a Greenwood girl.

They still won't talk about it, though. Not for the record, anyway. Even the one who quit the Sheriff's office and's back out there now, on his wife's land, trying to make a go of it.

The first still blames it on Stanton, that they were trying to get the Greenwood Rangers looking somewhere else instead of at the football game Friday night. But most of those players had grown up on farms themselves, would have been as physically unable as the rest of us to hold a match to their fathers' hopes and dreams.

The other deputy's best guess is just a version of that: kids. General mischief. Except there were no guilty tire tracks out there—three-wheelers, motorcycle, bikes, nothing. Not even horses.

But again, why? We could all see the run-away-fast fun of hitting one module, maybe, hear how earnest we would promise each other never to tell, no matter what. All of the modules, though—mostly King cotton, but some of Rooster's too, indirectly, and a couple of the narrow fields that were leased out between—to take the time to hit *all* of them, man.

Kids out drinking on a Wednesday night?

Not likely, deputy.

And then there were all the suspicious trucks that had evidently been bumper to bumper on Cloverdale that Wednesday just before dusk, too. A suspicious truck convention, more or less. None of them with their headlights on, all the men and pairs of men behind the wheel thoroughly sunglassed, ungrinning, there with dark purpose, with specific intent.

What would have been poetic, I think, though nobody hit on it, was if the family of whoever that was who'd turned up dead in 1963 had come back, had certain people in their targets. And a pocketful of matches.

Nobody in 1985 was thinking about twenty years ago, though, and that'd be movie-of-the-week stuff anyway. You'd have already heard about it by now.

Another possibility circulating fast and dangerous on Friday, even at school, was that some Mobil pumper'd had a blowout with his supervisor Wednesday morning then just blasted out to make his rounds anyway, never mind that he was fired. It was a thing of principle.

Some of those modules that burned, yeah, there was a pump road that ran alongside them.

And, if you don't know what being a pumper was about in 1985: all day you're in your truck, going to pad after pad, dragging a plume of caliche behind you, climbing those hot silver stairs, dropping your weighted tape down into the tank and reeling it back up slow, so you can record what the level is today. Then you write it in two logs—one in the box by the stairs, one in your truck—and you're off to the next one, and the next one.

It's not a bad job at all, and even in the mid-eighties lull, that slack between legitimate booms, there were still enough tanks that you could pull all the hours you wanted, pretty much. And, it had the distinct benefit of *not* being a roughnecking gig. Meaning you only worked in the daytime hours, and got to keep all your fingers, didn't have to have your big toes sewn onto where your thumbs used to be.

As for this particular pumper, Steve Grimes, the deputies finally caught up with him Friday afternoon, at the old Monterey's on the east side of Midland. He was sitting with some other oilfield guys, a pitcher of beer between them all, the table littered with chip baskets.

In the parking lot was his truck, red Pegasus horse and all, officially stolen now, along with the radio and some tools.

That was the least of his problems, though.

He'd evidently spent most of the time between the fight with his super and now driving out to every pumpjack in the county, and flipping their breakers. Not driving a bar through the circuits or draining the fluid out so they'd seize, but just turning them off, simple as that.

Though the ex-deputy who farms now—I'm not supposed to use his name, but come on—won't talk about the cotton fire or what came after, he will talk about arresting Steve Grimes that day, so long as I don't use any real names.

What "Steve Grimes" did was pull a chair out, slosh the pitcher over, invite the good old boys from the Sheriff's office to take a load off.

By then, because he'd still been using his company gas account, they knew he'd been through nearly four tanks. Making caliche loops back and forth, all over Midland county.

"You should know the pumps are back on," the other deputy told Steve Grimes.

"Just wanted a day off, yeah?" Grimes said back, lifting his beer for the other guys at his table to cheer in.

They leaned back, hissed smiles, found other places to rest their eyes.

They still had to work, I mean.

And it was easy as that. No fight, no tortilla chips flying onto other tables, no beer mugs thrown.

Finally, too—though we wouldn't know this until just after our quiet, quiet Christmas—the electric company was able to clear Grimes. Caprock Electric, out of Stanton, who still had most of the rural contracts in the eastern part of Midland County back then, and over into Martin.

The night of the fire, Steve Grimes had been way east, throwing breakers on pumpjacks. The meters confirmed what he'd written in the logs. He might have been a fired pumper, but he was still a pumper, I guess, unable to keep his nub of a pencil out of all those lined pages.

After he was cleared, then, that left us back where we'd started: Tommy Moore. A possibility that had surfaced for a bit, early on, in relation to all the shady trucks in the area—every time there's a bad wreck in Greenwood, there are always suspicious trucks and cars everywhere. A friend of mine even used one to explain a three-wheeler crash he had, one that left a line of scar tissue smiling inches back from each side of his mouth (barbed wire). Another friend I got in a fight with, just because somebody'd seen a car the color of his on the same road one of my cousins was bleeding out on.

Nobody liked this story, though. The one with Tommy Moore still in it.

But what else was there?

***

To start at the beginning, it was early December. So, just why *wasn't* Tommy Moore at school that morning? I can hear a particular mom in a kitchen in 1985, coffee on the table before her, a cigarette permanently clamped between her fingers like the least important thing, saying this to her friend across the table but leaning close too, like it's an obvious, obvious secret: "Why *wasn't* he up at the school, though?"

It's not something the men would have thought about. Just because it made perfect sense to them, putting tractor work before school work. Which of the two was actually going to get you somewhere, right?

Tommy Moore wasn't planning on staying around Greenwood, though. He already had a letter from Midland Junior College, was going to be a Chaparral, let basketball buy him a couple more years of school. It's what his big brother was doing already, just with the military instead of sports, guns instead of basketballs.

But he never had Tommy's jump shot, either. Nobody did. That way he had of just blocking out the world, focusing only on that orange rim, no matter what hammer the other team had put on the floor just to show him how hard he could get nailed for every two points he drained.

Could we have gone all the way to the state tournament his senior year, if Rob King hadn't plowed his face into the ground?

Nobody said it out loud, but we all knew.

Teams like that happen once every ten years, if that. Returning seniors with a star to lead them.

No, that next year, all of us who were old enough to be out in the fields alone but still too young to drive stripper, we'd get posted out by the modules. Guards. Our orders: not to confront, just run off, identify later.

Which is just to say it again: nobody knew who'd done it last time. For all anybody knew, that firestarter could still be out there, striking matches in a darkened room. Waiting for the right night.

And our moms hated it, of course, putting us out there like that, but they understood. Were proud of us the way I guess moms who send their uniformed sons overseas must feel. All the moms that year were Mrs. Moore, yeah.

Except of course these moms, our moms, they could bring us dinner still hot in its foil, and we'd pretend we didn't want it, didn't need it, but then would keep them there too long all the same, just talking about nothing. Asking them questions about when they were girls.

You always look for the moment you grew up, I think. Like it's a thing that happens all at once.

But sometimes it is.

For me it wasn't standing guard that next year, but my mom shaking me from bed one morning, my brothers still asleep, my dad already gone. What had happened was our year-old cat, still a kitten herself, had had a kitten. Just the one. But it was all wrong—no hair, not-yet-finished eyes. Just there on the concrete stairs that led to our screen door, breathing fast and shallow. Its mom watching it from the cinderblock fence, unconcerned.

I put on my basketball shorts and my favorite boots, the tallest ones I had, and scooped the broken thing into a shovel, carried it to the burn barrel, and, because a gunshot would send the horses through the fence, finally just raised a stray cinderblock over my head, held it there for what I know's too long, and brought it down as hard as I've ever done anything.

My mule-ear boots went to my knees, almost, were still too big, hand-me-downs, but they weren't quite tall enough, either. My thighs got misted, coated, sprayed.

And then it was just breakfast, school, the usual. Nobody even knowing. My mom never asked, I mean. It was how I knew I was grown up: I had things inside me that weren't for anybody else. Things I'd have to carry from here on out.

Was that what it was like for Tommy Moore that morning, looking up at Rob King's fists?

If that particular mom smoking her cigarette knew so much, she should have just told us all who did it, who started those fires.

Then none of the rest of this would have happened.

***

Why wasn't Tommy Moore at school that morning?

If I could find him anymore, or knew anybody who'd kept up—he's in Austin, maybe?—this is what I'm pretty sure he'd say: that it wasn't about the three and a quarter he was going to get for another hour of work. No, the reason he stayed on that morning, it had a lot more to do with what he was missing. What he would have paid to miss.

In Greenwood that year, there weren't enough coaches to go around. If you weren't a three-sport player—we were 3A, but just barely—then you'd pretty much get ignored. Especially, say, if the whole school was gearing up for a game that had been rained out in October, a game with the Buffaloes, natural enemy to the Greenwood Ranger.

It hadn't always been like that, though, the hostility. In my dad and uncles' time, Greenwood had just been a kindergarten through sixth grade affair. That sounds small, but compared to what used to be there, what my great-grandfather had pointed out to me one afternoon, it was an industrial complex, a series of buildings nobody could have predicted. What my great-grandfather pointed out to me was where Prairie Lee used to be. A one-room school, the only one between Midland and Stanton, the same way Midland was halfway between Dallas and El Paso. Prairie Lee was just a dull rise in the pasture now. My great-grandfather held his finger there for longer than he needed to, like he was maybe trying to see it as it had been. Long enough for me to see it, anyway. And I wouldn't forget. A few years later, when that land was being developed, I'd be at a sleepover with a friend who lived next to that pasture and I'd sneak out after everybody was crashed, feel my way through the fence, see if there was anything to find of Prairie Lee. There wasn't.

That same year, though, following a different fence in a different pasture, I would find an old shack that looked like I imagined Prairie Lee had. Except instead of shattered chalkboards or old desks there would be beer bottles and bean cans, and, on one wall, more intricate than any blueprint I've ever seen, a pencil drawing of the floor plan of some holding unit—a jail or prison, I never knew. I left as quietly as I'd come in, kept following the fence, finally and unaccountably finding a bottle of Mennen aftershave on its side by the base of a locust post. Like it had just fallen from the sky. For me.

I knew what it was, what aftershave was, but I had to trade for what I'd seen in that shack, too.

I twisted the lid off, closed my eyes, and drank it all down at once, didn't let myself throw it back up.

The way I know it worked is that whoever was staying there, or had been staying there, they never came for me, or my family.

Maybe that was a shed we all went to, though. We just never said anything about it to each other.

Maybe Tommy Moore's big brother had even been there years ago, but not found the right way to cancel it out, had just walked by whatever bottle had been placed there for him. Whatever stray loop of barbed wire he could have cut himself on if he'd known. Cut himself deep, or shallow, in even lines above the hem of his sleeve, on the thigh just above the frayed bottom of a pair of jean shorts.

I don't know, would never ask him something that stupid, if anybody even knew where he was.

Because—what if he shrugged, looked away, *did* know that shed?

Either way, it went bad for Tommy.

The reason he had an extra hour to kill on the stripper that morning, it was that athletics was first period, and he didn't play football. There were six of them that year who didn't get fitted for jocks and helmets, no matter who pulled them out of class, talked to them. Not just coaches but cheerleaders, cheerleaders on game day in their short blue skirts, their eyes painted to match.

The reason: the year before, playing in Stanton, word had gotten over to Greenwood that if 30 got the ball even once, he was going to be leaving the field on a stretcher.

It was the usual intimidation game, but then it wasn't.

Second quarter, 30 got the ball, went wide around the side where his speed could get him some room.

The Buffaloes were ready, though. Choreographed, even. At least that's how it looked from the visitors' stands.

30 hit one of them straight-on, and that Buffalo—this is what everybody focused on later, how that lineman outweighed our 30 by a good sixty pounds—that Buffalo let himself be thrown back, enough that 30 extended up at an angle, almost to his full length, like all he was trying to do here anymore was hold the ball down, keep it from floating away.

In came the cornerback head first, aiming for 30's armpit. Spearing him.

People in the stands were crying, I remember. Some of the dads who had been high-schoolers at Stanton themselves, they were stiff-legging it out to the parking lot, their faces set, their hands already held in the shape of whatever they were going to thread out from behind their seat, wrench up from the bed of their truck. Their wives who had known them in high school following, holding onto them as they tried to walk back.

Like Stanton had promised, 30 left on a stretcher, and we lost the game, and 30 was out for the rest of the season, only came back midway through basketball.

The players who were on that team with him, they remembered how nervous he was about contact at first, so that when two-a-days started up in August, they stayed in their driveways shooting free throws. Concentrating on their form. Their sweet tea over there in the shade, the radio in their truck on, windows down. Their girlfriends just a phone call away.

Their punishment, of course, was offseason basketball.

All it was was running.

One of the coaches (Fidel, a real name) would sometimes sit in a plastic orange chair to watch, but that was only if football was getting a lecture that day.

Usually, the day's work would be on the chalkboard in the locker room: *Second pump behind the Evans', TWICE.*

Instead of running around the track, taunting the football players crab-crawling out there like soldiers, the basketball team had to *run*, not lollygag (Fidel's favorite word, after "yahoos"), through the cotton field next to the school. All the way to the second pumpjack, the one two miles off.

You couldn't cut it short, either, even if everyone agreed not to say anything.

At unpredictable times, Coach Fidel would take one of the teachers' cars, sneak past the back way by the water station, and be waiting behind the angle-iron rail of the pumpjack, just flicking the power switch on and off like he didn't have anything better to do.

Running through cotton, too, especially all through November and into December, it's like wading through line after line of shrubs, like you've been sent to hell and it turns out hell's a plant nursery. You can vault over for the first quarter-mile or so, if you get the rhythm right, but pretty soon your toes start catching the top of the plant, and by the time you're through your first wind your shoes are stained wet green again. Never mind that Rooster, who farms the field, knows the head coach, and says he's going to take it out of somebody's skin if his bolls are all knocked off. Never mind that the dirt, cool under the shade of the cotton, is soft and deep, and that unless you catch the upsloping wall of the next furrow just right, your ankle's probably going to grind against itself, make you very aware your Achilles tendon is a rubber band, one that's only got so many stretches in it.

All of which is to say that Tommy Moore, he had good reason to skip first period. Especially with the legitimate excuse of helping a booster, a deacon, an ex-school board member, get the cotton out of his field.

However, a legitimate excuse to a coach is a good reason to get razzed as well. Especially from a pack of guys dripping green from their feet.

The turnrow Tommy Moore was in that morning with Ms. Godfrey (I can't call her Sheryl, never knew her as a Ledbetter), it was really Rooster's turnrow, about forty feet outside the last rut Rooster's circle system had carved into the ground all season. Just winter wheat matted down there, from the buggy getting pulled back and forth.

It wasn't that Rooster would just let anybody use his turnrow, but the quarter-section his circle irrigated, it was land he'd bought from a King cousin. Land he'd outbid King *for*. So there was that. And, sure, in somebody else's field, you can drive over a riser on accident—that's why you don't want just anybody there—but nobody would ever just leave that riser bubbling either. If you break it, you fix it, no questions asked. And it's not like you can use up a turnrow, anyway. They're made to do donuts in.

Since 1985, that field of Rooster's that ran alongside King's has changed a lot, so there's no way to tell anymore if you're walking where it all happened or not. No way to tell if you should be feeling anything. Rooster's field, even, it's in development now, was too tempting, right across from the school like that. He wasn't stupid when he bid, I mean.

Back then, too, we could have gone out there on our three-wheelers, touched the ground with our fingers, imagined we were touching dried blood. But then we'd have to see the burned-down modules as well. All of them, like an army had come through, left destruction in its wake, just smoldering piles. And we could get a rush from imagining dried blood on the pads of our fingers, sure. But that ash from the cotton. We knew better than to bring that home.

From the road now, anyway, you can see the old pad where the second pumpjack used to be, before the Permian Basin collapsed in the nineties. How close it seems to the school, too. How stupid we were back then.

And, no, that pack of offseason basketball players running that morning, I wasn't one of them. Wasn't old enough for junior varsity yet, even. But I can talk about it because I had to run just the same when I came up. The only difference was that now one of the coaches always had to pace us over on Cloverdale. Sometimes in his own car, the hazard lights on, sometimes in somebody's truck. Close enough that we could all see his window down, his breath smoky.

And that's what it was about, too: cigarettes.

When you're sixteen, even if you don't smoke, you do.

Sure, we'd all dipped our way through elementary, thumbing the cans into the seat pockets of our Wranglers then praying for that faded circle to appear, that badge that proved we didn't do *every*thing our moms told us. Rubbing concrete into the shiny lids then bending snips of coat hangers into the concrete, so that we'd get belt buckles that would last a week if we didn't cinch our belts too tight. Sneaking our dads' whiskey a drop at a time into our cans so we could act tipsy from the nicotine buzz, let everybody smell our breath. But now that we were starting to discover pool—some of the dads had mid-life pool tables in their bricked-over garages, and didn't get a summer vacation like we did—smoking was the cool thing. We all wanted that cigarette hanging casual from the corner of our mouths as we lined up a shot. Wanted to have to squint through the smoke like tough guys. It was practice for who we were all planning to be.

But that morning, none of the offseason basketball guys would have rolled a pack into their socks. It would have gotten beat to death against the cotton.

Tommy, though, working. Of *course* he'd have some, right?

It would have been a gamble, angling over to the stripper instead of the pumpjack, but sometimes a cigarette's worth whatever else might happen. Too, if your lungs are already on fire, why *not* have smoke coming out your mouth, right?

So that's the story that started Friday, got upstaged by Steve Grimes, but was still there after Grimes had been cleared.

Nobody knew who, exactly—nobody wanted to be that person—but there was word that when the first fire trucks arrived on the scene from Stanton, that, between those slow-smoking modules and the school, running through the cotton like ghosts, far enough away already that they looked motionless almost, was a pack of six offseason basketball players, their hands in fists by their sides, not even one of them looking back.

And I wish I could leave them there like that too.

Chapter Three

In the GHS yearbook from '85/'86, Ms. Godfrey is looking slightly out of frame. Like there's something happening just behind the camera.
 Ms. Godfrey.
 Sheryl Ledbetter.
 At first I didn't even look in the L's for her.
 Worse, when I'm waiting in the main office, she remembers me. Doesn't even break stride, just steps past the desk, wraps her arms around my neck. Has to stand up on one foot to do it.
 I smile, don't know what to do with my hands.
 "You made it," she whispers into my shoulder, and now I don't know what to do with my eyes either.
 Instead of talking to me there, she takes me to the library, to my Dewey Decimal number. All my books are there. All the ones I never sent her.
 I made it.
 I don't feel right in the teacher's lounge—I only ever snuck in there once, for nothing remotely wholesome—so we walk the carpeted halls at four-thirty after school, my hands deep in my pockets.
 "Ms. Everett," I say, passing one of the three labs. Another real name.

Ms. Godfrey nods, looks pleasantly ahead of us, her lips held slightly different now, I think. As far as I know, she never knew Ms. Everett—Ms. Everett was both after and before Ms. Godfrey—but probably heard about the memorial service (the funeral was in Arkansas, where she was from). Ms. Everett, who had a seizure while ironing one morning before school, died like that. I got in a fight with a good friend about her the next day, still carry a scar on my back where he threw me into a paper towel rack in the cafeteria bathroom, the back of my shirt so bloody I had to wear a football jersey the rest of the day like I had spirit, rah rah, because the basketball jerseys didn't have sleeves. My friend had probably just said her name wrong, I don't know. Or probably he'd just said it at all. If she'd made it to school that day, though, then Coach Sharpe wouldn't have been asked to finish her class for her—he had a B.S. in something, so maybe knew what a Bunsen burner was—and his Senior English wouldn't have needed a semester-long substitute. One still finishing her degree.

Ms. Godfrey.

We were all taller than her, I remember.

And English, it was supposed to be a joke. Sharpe's English had been, anyway. All you had to do was prod him with the right questions and he'd pinch his polyester shorts up to sit on his desk and tell stories all period. Show us his fingers, how crooked they were from his wide receiver days. Tell us about his year on the motocross circuit, before he was married. It was a joke, fifth period. Right after lunch, after—if it wasn't basketball season—we would have all been out in the parking lot, bottles stashed under the seats of our trucks, our jackets still exhaling smoke every time we moved.

Deal was, though, Ms. Godfrey, she'd been in that same parking lot just four years ago.

If I would have been one year older, I probably would have remembered her senior year. She'd be a face at the pep rallies, anyway; not out on the court, with pompoms, but one of the ones in the stands, going through the motions, waiting this thing out. Going on the yearbook photos, that's what I'd guess her senior year was about. She's not in Future Homemakers, isn't a sweetheart for FFA, isn't in any of the language or science clubs (or auto or meat judging), didn't compete in UIL's Number Sense, and didn't get voted most anything or show up in nostalgic silhouette at the bonfire. After what Pete Manson told me, it makes sense: she was spending all her extra hours at the hospital, tending to Tommy Moore. And then, when he was home, she was over there nursing him, threading his bangs back behind an ear, lying to him that it was all going to be all right, that nothing had to change.

If you ask me, Ms. Godfrey and Tommy Moore should have been Homecoming King and Queen that year. Retroactively. Prom royalty as well. Mr. and Mrs. Everything, forever.

Instead, I think everybody kind of just pretended they weren't there. Because if they *were* there in the halls, at the bonfires, in the stands, then they'd have to think about the rest—the fire, the trial, the guns, all of it.

It's the crowd version of what finally pulled the two of them apart, I'd guess: Tommy, unable to look at her and not see her on top of the module that morning, screaming for Rob King to stop.

But I can't ask her about that now, of course. If I ask what broke them up, then she'll have to think about what if they didn't, what if she'd stayed with him even though he was pushing her away, what if, like all the songs said she was supposed to, she'd stood by him?

Would he be lost down in Austin now?

If there were some way to just get this from the yearbook, I mean, believe me, that's where I'd be. No offense, Ms. Godfrey, please. And I'm not ready to talk to Pete Manson again either, yet. I don't want to have to see her through his eyes.

Just the facts, as far as I know them.

At college in Abilene, Sheryl Ledbetter met Roger Godfrey, who I don't really know except to raise a finger to over my steering wheel. He's about twelve years older than her, would have been a senior when she was just starting kindergarten. I can't imagine they met in class one day at Hardin-Simmons, or that one of her friends introduced them.

You have to admit, though, his wiry mustache, his suit: he's not Tommy, not who Tommy was going to grow into. Probably doesn't ever even remind her.

But this book's going to be on that shelf in the school library too, I know.

I'll never see it, never sign it. Don't want her (you, Ms. Godfrey, I'm sorry) to have to pretend she didn't read this. To hug me again like I haven't betrayed her, and everybody.

So.

What I Remember Best About Her Senior English.

This is my report.

What I remember best is that we gave her hell at first, until the principal had to come talk to us, her out in the hall, sure she'd done the wrong thing, calling in the brass. What I remember is the way our girlfriends and ex-girlfriends—this being all of the girls, yeah—would cut their eyes at us every time Godfrey turned to diagram a sentence on the board. What I remember is that she actually made us read and take quizzes on *Red Badge of Courage* and *Heart of Darkness* and *The Great Gatsby*, and *Catcher in the Rye* and *The Last Picture Show*, even though the librarian kept the copies of those last two behind the desk. And don't worry, this isn't some cornball light going off in my head, this life I'm in now suddenly taking shape ahead of me.

No.

But there was something.

To keep us from leering at her, Godfrey started wearing frumpier and frumpier clothes, her oldest sister's I'd guess, so that we'd forget she was only five years ahead of us. I felt sorry for her for that, in a dull way. Like I knew I should be feeling sorry for her and wished I were doing it better. Or, I missed the way she'd been those first few weeks, anyway. Maybe selfishly. It made her a joke for the girls, too, the way she started dressing. But it's not like we could stand up for her. We needed those girls, I mean. All we needed from Godfrey was a passing grade so we'd be eligible to play.

But because I didn't like what she was doing to herself, what we were making her do to herself, I slipped.

She figured out I could read. Aloud.

In Coach Roarke's seventh grade life science, I'd always been the one who would read aloud at the end of class. Just because I could zip through a chapter in no time, and not miss a word. It was a joke, then.

Not to Godfrey.

We were reading *Beowulf* one week, going down the row, taking turns stumbling through the lines and when it was my turn—and after Michelle, the girl to my right, had shown me what page we were on, Michelle who had just been pointing out Godfrey's barely too-long slip to another girl, maybe Kelly, then flaring her eyes and holding them wide like that—I pushed her Ranger-blue fingernail farther out of the way than I had to and fell right into the lope of that translation, pronounced all of those old words right, stresses, sentence breaks, all of it, like I'd been practicing all week. Not like this was my first time to open that chapter of our book.

When I was done, ready to hand-off, it was quiet instead. Ms. Godfrey clapped.

I smiled, wouldn't look at her, but was suddenly the designated reader again, until in the locker room the guys were thou'ing and thee'ing me. Like I'd been reading the Bible in class, not Old English.

Ms. Godfrey didn't turn me on to reading, to writing—blame my uncle for that—but she did make me realize I was different. That I wasn't like anybody else in that locker room.

You made it, she'd told me, her eyes closed against my shoulder, all her weight on the back of my neck, only one foot on the ground.

Thank you.

***

"Pete, right?" she says to me after we've walked all the halls, my hand darting out at one point to touch the metal of my old locker, then the one two down from it. Where we are now is outside, the east side of the school, the south corner of what's still the new part to me. It's where Mr. Brenhemin's shop class stood to watch the fire that morning.

There's young trees planted all around now, each with plaques I haven't read yet, each with garden-hose-wrapped cable tying them down at three points. Against the wind. So they won't be on Michael Graham's next list.

I nod yes to her, that Pete told me.

She does her lips like she's been expecting him to tell somebody, it's just been a matter of time, then produces a pack of cigarettes from some pocket of her dress.

It's like catching your preacher holding a centerfold with one hand.

"Pete the Rabbit," she says, not really to me, I don't think, cupping her hand around the flame.

It's what everybody used to call him, from the pattern he planted his cotton. I can't remember exactly what it was now—there's only so many variations with an eight-row planter—but I do remember that that's always how you knew it was a Pete Manson field: the way he'd hop this row, or that one, nothing symmetrical. All his plows fitted for it, like he wanted to be sure nobody else could work his cotton but him. Like he knew his equipment was all going on the auction block soon, and he wanted to inconvenience whoever stole it.

Ms. Godfrey doesn't offer me a cigarette. That would be the worst thing ever.

How old I am here is thirty-six.

What I want to say, note out loud, is that she didn't used to smoke. We would have smelled it on her, would have seen her out by the doors with the other teachers, the High Bun Club, the Cat Eye Crew. What I want to say is she's doing this in remembrance, to honor Tommy. To go back to that morning again, smoke all around, and somehow step out of it in a different place.

What I say instead is that those houses didn't used to be there like that, in Rooster's field. Did they?

She inhales, holds it.

"Your brother?" she asks, almost like she's afraid what I might have to say.

He had her for English too, three years after I did.

For a while he was famous in Greenwood for lying on Cloverdale at night, on the yellow road stripes in front of the church, letting the cars blast by on either side. He was in sixth grade then, still had a lot of years left to luck his way through.

I tell her where he's living, what he's doing.

She narrows her eyes each time she inhales, the make-up by her eyes not quite moving with the skin.

"I'm a character," she finally says, looking over at me.

In one of my books.

I shrug.

"You're not going to use my real name?"

"I'm changing them all."

"And Tommy?"

"He's somebody else too."

She nods, says, "That's about true, yeah."

"Ms. Godfrey—"

"What did Pete say?"

I start to tell her, know I'm going to get it wrong and scrape something open between them, so I pull my truck around, the sole of my boot skating over the asphalt, gravel dancing up against my rocker panel.

She reads the Pete part on my laptop, me blocking the sun, her blowing the dust from the screen, my hair in my eyes, but maybe that's best.

"How'd you get home from the airport?" she asks.

"He got it right, then?" I ask back.

"You used his real name."

"Not both of them."

She clicks the laptop closed, keeps the lid down with her fingers. It's something I haven't ever seen anybody do before.

"You should be careful, you know," she finally says.

"I'm changing some of the dates too."

"It's enough?"

We both know it's not.

All around the school grounds now are houses. Baby Jessica used to live in one of them. A Texas Ranger in another.

On one of the roads winding through the houses, when the houses were still just frames and tar paper, I jumped off a hay ride once, didn't make the ditch, scratched the face off the cowboy on my belt buckle but got up and kept running, only fell down behind one of the houses, knees bloody, palms raw. Halloween. No clue why I jumped either. All that's left is the brief flash of a girl I liked then. She's singing a Tiffany song with all the other girls.

What I want to tell Ms. Godfrey but know I won't is that the first story I ever got noticed for, the first full-length story I ever wrote, it was "West Texas Dirt." About this dad out beside a tractor, snakebit, dying, planting a sunflower weed back into the ground, his daughter seeing the whole field yellow two months later, and knowing it's for her.

It's the stupidest story.

No farmer would ever do that.

Even when you see one of them up from a week down in McAllen or somewhere—funeral, wedding, cheap feed, whatever—they'll always have some absolute *tree* of a cotton stalk in the back of their truck, but that's all it'll ever be. Never the leaves, the squares, the bolls. The stalk rubbed shiny even, likely with a gas rag, because nobody—and I mean *nobody*—wants to be the one to introduce some new brand of weevil to West Texas.

But those contraband stalks. I remember old guys looking both ways down Cloverdale then pulling that ridiculously tall plant out from behind their bench seats, half hiding it behind their door just in case some county agent's got them in a pair of binoculars.

They're holy relics, giant compared to our cotton, the elder gods of what we raise. And then you burn them in the barrels, get back to real life.

That's what I should have written about in that first story, I think. Then I could have stepped out in a different place as well. The way you can stand in a young field in July and watch all the new leaves for hundreds of acres around you turn as one, following the sun? How, after the cropduster's come, you can find these little dying owls out in the cotton, then carry them around all day in the truck with you, their yellow eyes just watching you the whole time? How terrifying it is your first time pulling a knifing rig, even though you're just learning on hay grazer, so it doesn't really count? How sometimes you can get thirsty enough to drink from the handlines, even though you've dug burst-open skunks and rabbits from those same pipes? How in a field that's just been baled up, you can stand there after the tractor's gone and hear the rattlesnakes buzzing in the square bales?

Or, no.

What I should have written about is the transmission of my first truck. How it kept slipping, had nearly three-hundred-thousand miles on it already. But there's a trick to that, too: eek two drops of brake fluid down that bent tube and the rubber seals all tighten up, you'll get better pressure, and bam, assuming you've spitballed the vacuum modulator and taken a ball-peen hammer to your carrier bearing, you've got a smooth ride, with shifts that'll throw you back in the seat a little, for the first few days at least.

It worked for my truck, anyway.

My friend, though.

He had a mid-seventies Ford like mine, so we figured the brake fluid would work for his truck as well. We were sixteen; me and my mom and brothers were living in a trailer in the middle of a pecan orchard that year. Specifically, watching *Dirty Dancing* on VHS, a movie I've still never seen to the end.

The reason is that those two drops didn't work for my friend's transmission. So he figured two more might be the ticket, then two more. Pretty soon it was half a quart and his transmission spun out, wouldn't even pretend to grab.

His dad found this out about seven-thirty, just before dinner. That the truck he'd just bought for his undeserving son was junk now.

For thirty minutes he banged around the shop cussing, counting his rods and losing count each time, and when he finally came out again, it was after my friend, who I'm not going to name here. First it was just fists, some kicking, my friend all over their caliche drive, nothing new, but then he made the mistake of running out into the pasture, away from his dad's steel toes.

I picture him, my friend's dad, standing in the floodlight, glaring into that darkness, then walking away himself.

Next: headlights in the pasture, everywhere. My friend's dad after him with the welding truck.

By the time my friend made it to our trailer six miles away, it was ten-thirty, and he was torn and bleeding and limping; his dad had caught him once with the bumper, sent him rolling. Waited for him to get up before coming after him again, great roostertails of dirt geysering up behind him, pelting the roof of the house they were still building and would be for a few years yet.

We kept him that night, and then the cops were there in three cars and I didn't see him again for two years. By then his arms were nothing but scar tissue. Not from needles, but from the metal teeth that keep Ace bandages together.

Locked up, all his shoestrings and belts and pants taken away, he'd figured out he could still cut himself with those little teeth.

It's a trick I would learn too, without him.

Maybe like that shed, though, it's something everybody figures out for a while. That they can trade. That you can always trade.

And what I didn't tell you about reading for Ms. Godfrey my senior year, what I didn't want to say, it's that once, going through *Gawain* or *Gilgamesh*—something with a G—it got to where I could hear my voice separate from myself, like another person altogether, and it was then that I knew I shouldn't have done what I'd just been doing out in the parking lot, over lunch.

I knew if I held onto my desk, everything would be fine, nobody would know. Except then I was holding onto my desk and the carpet was on the side of my face too, a scratchy red and grey weave I can still feel, and I was trying to speak, to read, and probably was, except Ms. Godfrey was shrieking across the classroom for me, cradling my head into her lap, onto her hand-me-down skirt.

It was history all over again for her, I know now.

Just how she'd wanted to hold Tommy Moore, when she thought he was dying.

***

I should get Rob King and Tommy Moore's dad out of that road now.

My best friend from elementary's big sister knows the story of it, kind of, and told us once when she was supposed to just be watching us. These were the years she was still in a leg cast from their family's big car wreck in Midland. I never saw her walk without crutches until years after I'd last talked to her brother. I didn't even recognize her. It's one of those things I should be able to write better, make real, watching her glide past in a department store, how I felt everything shift around me, like I was in some slightly alternate Midland, Texas now, some charmed, accidental place.

She was still beautiful, of course. The way she held the tips of her fingers together now that she didn't have to be gripping foam handles. How happy her hands were.

I'd been in elementary-school love with her for a while, ever since she let us listen to her Prince record but lifted the needle at certain times, so as not to corrupt us.

Janna.

That's pretty much her real name, sorry. What she told us about what happened over on 1120 that day though, it's no secret.

She wasn't sitting in some window spying on all of Greenwood either, her crutches leaned up against the window. From her house, all you can see is an old buffalo wallow and a flash of blacktop past it.

No, the reason she kind of saw what happened was that she'd been coming back from town with her mom, one of her doctor appointments. Their long driveway started maybe twenty yards past where Arthur King was parked half in the ditch, half not, his door open.

Janna was sitting in the back seat, of course, and knew so, so well not to run her leg alongside the driver's seat anymore. Now she sat in the middle, her crutches beside her, stickers all up and down the wood.

I don't even want to write this.

But. But they stopped, her and her mom, could each see Arthur King stepping from his truck, levering his seat forward, extracting the 870 he kept back there. Not the 16 gauge Belgium-made Browning Auto 5—you don't let a gun like that bounce around behind your seat, don't even let your grandkids ever shoot it—but the old pump he carried. Not for moments like these, I wouldn't imagine, but still: it worked.

He planted the butt against his thigh, angled it up into the sky, away from any transformer or utility pole, and, according to Janna, looked right into their car when he pulled the trigger. So they'd understand that they had nothing to be scared of, here. That this gun wasn't for them.

Janna's mom, too, that day of their accident, she'd seen some things it's not my place to mention, so, no, she didn't go hysterical, start screaming. And Janna, she was in ninth grade that year. She just watched.

In the silence the shotgun left, Tommy Moore's dad rose up from Rob King, cut his eyes across the distance, to Arthur King.

Arthur King didn't angle the gun down at him, but he didn't cock it behind his shoulder either.

As for what they said, I have no clue; Janna's mom had the heater blowing, the windows all up.

Or maybe he didn't even say anything. Because it was all already right there: *What you're doing for your son, I'll do that too. Please.*

It's not something Arthur King would ever say out loud.

After a few breaths, Tommy Moore's dad nodded, looked back down to the bloodied ball of Rob King, and turned around.

Except—Janna had seen *Terminator* I don't know how many times by then—behind him, Rob King stood, somehow.

This wasn't any movie, though.

Tommy Moore's dad felt Rob King standing, or maybe Rob King said something, or breathed wrong. Either way, Tommy Moore's dad turned around, not sure what Rob King wanted.

More?

When your son's that deep in the hospital, I mean, you've always got more.

But that wasn't it.

Rob King set his mouth, stepped forward, almost into Tommy Moore's dad, his own dad calling something out to him but he ignored it.

He leaned into the side of Tommy Moore's dad's truck, grabbed onto the shop-made bed rail with both hands, and closed his eyes, lowered his head, then came up again, turned to face Tommy Moore's dad. For, in Janna's words, "forever, almost."

She was kind of right, too. I can still see him there.

Locked up for two days, two nights, he'd had the time to think about what had happened. What he'd done.

Finally, he looked away, down to his right hand, the one still bloody-knuckled, and, with his left, popped Tommy Moore's dad's toolbox open. The hatch gull-winged up, bounced once or twice.

"What?"

It's what Tommy's Moore's dad must have said.

This: Rob King placing his hand there on the corner of the open toolbox, then, before anybody could stop, Janna's mom only realizing it at the last moment, diving between the seats to block Janna's view, Rob King brought that lid down with all the weight he had left, harder than he'd ever hit Tommy Moore.

The lid came down far enough to catch, broke his hand bad enough for three surgeries that still left it wrong.

It would be another two days before Arthur King made it home with his son.

***

Ms. Godfrey—it's an Old English derivation of a name, see?—doesn't tell me any of this, of course. It's legend. And if Janna was the main source of it all, then good for her. When you're on crutches for six years, you need to be the one with the best story.

And if she made it up, then good for her still.

Rob King's surgeries that spring were real, anyway. But maybe you can get three surgeries in your hand just from hitting somebody in the face over and over.

It's not the kind of thing you can ask a person, really.

If this were some other book, too, there would likely be an X-ray here of Rob King's hand. Or if those are all gone by now, I could probably even sub one of mine in—by the time I was twenty I'd broke my right hand three times, the bones in there gravel now, boxer's fracture over and over—but that's all it would be: the shadow of flesh around a confusion of bone. At first you wouldn't know it was a hand, even, until you cued into the light dusting of arm hair, the empty space of the fingernails. What had to have happened to have done this.

But this isn't that book.

What I have is this, Ms. Godfrey and me standing just around the side of the high school.

"Does it change anything?" she's saying to me.

I kind of huff air out my nose, I guess.

It's no answer.

"Pete saying you were there?" I tag on, half in apology.

She nods.

I swallow.

"You and Tommy," I say, not looking at her now.

"He was beautiful back then," she says.

I've seen him in the yearbook, in his short eighties shorts, the segmented glass wall of the gym behind him, his mouth held in a way that you can tell the only thing in the world for him right then is that orange rim ten feet up.

It's what we all want, to exist like that, so deep in the moment that that moment never stops dilating out and out. Like being inside a balloon forever inflating. That sound of fullness. That *feel*.

"But Taylor and Dwayne and the rest," I try, eyes narrowed to be saying their names out loud like this.

Taylor O'Hara, Dwayne Roberts, and the other offseason basketball players.

"Trevor and Tad and Marcus and Geoff...Geoff Koenig," Ms. Godfrey says, grinding her cigarette out in the Diet Dr. Pepper can she already had out here, twisted into the grass. "The Three T's."

There's a yearbook photo of them the following year, hamming it up by the ball racks, their arms out beside them, three letter T's.

Three, not four.

And—I've gone back, studied like it's a test—the reason she tagged Geoff's last name on like that is that there was another Jeff who graduated with her. Jeff Tarpley.

"You're just going to have to ask me," she says, calling me by name, looking over at me until I have to turn, face her.

Early, early on, kindergarten for me, maybe, one of the times we'd come back to Greenwood, I got led out into a field in late April, when the fields were all white crust and heat.

What I was supposed to see was how all the cotton, the whole crop, it was all kneeling there just under that white crust. That all you had to do was scratch it open and the plant would stand up, delicate and white-green.

I spent the rest of that day out there, scratching careful little holes.

"Did they do it?" I manage to say to her, real casual, like it doesn't even matter.

Ms. Godfrey looks back to the field where the houses are now.

She's about to cry, I can tell.

I won't know what to do if she does.

Run, get the principal? Light her another cigarette?

What she's thinking, I know: that it's all her fault.

And that's what I'm really asking, under the tangle of facts, which never really matter anyway: why did it have to happen like it did?

"I didn't tell," she says.

"I won't write any of this down," I tell her.

She laughs. Her shoulders hitch up once, anyway. I study a brown and bronze plaque angled under a young tree.

"You have to write it down," she says, looking over to me, her not-grey-yet hair blowing across her face. "That's why—it's why I got you, right?"

"Got me?"

"Things always fix themselves," she says, "always come back around, don't you know?"

And then she tells me.

***

When I don't believe her, I drive back out to Pete Manson's but then just sit on the road by his place, the sun angling down, the shadows of all his trees stretching towards me.

After a while he sees my truck, stands on his porch smoking a cigarette, makes a production of dropping it, of grinding it into the dirt. Of going back inside, the screen door flapping behind him.

I ease away, burn two days digging up Marcus Weeks, the 1986 team's point guard. He's a car salesman on the other side of Midland now, still favors his ribs on the left side, thinks I'm interested in buying at first but then makes me somehow. Shakes his head. Shrugs yes to what of Ms. Godfrey's story I tell him—her and them and Pete that day by the stripper—but adds some too, like he thought I already knew. Like of everybody, I should be the one to have already known this.

It's why Ms. Godfrey never told. Why she never had to tell.

That section across from the school, across from the church, that the basketball players had to run through for offseason, it had been broken up into fourths a generation ago. Like all the other sections had been when Arthur King's dad Walter King, Jr. died, and the black cars stretched for half a mile down 307. They were quartered up because Walter Jr. had four kids—Arthur, Arthur's older brother Walter III, dead in World War II, and two sisters, who only existed through the mail and in other people's photo albums anymore, like black-and-white secrets. The King land had still been all together at Walter Jr.'s death because Walter Jr. had been the only one of his five brothers and sisters to go into the family business, to lay claim to the land by working it, inherit it from his father, the first Walter, "Walt," who bought the land from the railroad or something, arrowheads and all. So, once Walter Jr. died, the land was quartered up section by section to the four kids, even though the one Walter Jr. had been gambling on was dead. It was supposed to be the most fair way to do it, so if one plot were more prime than the next, then each would get a part of that. And they'd also each get a quarter of the dryland, some of it up to thirty miles away. As for the dead brother's quarter-sections, Arthur absorbed them into his own. Maybe he got his sisters to sign off on it somehow, in spite of their own husbands' advice, farmers themselves in other counties, or maybe, because he was the brother, and the oldest, he could just say that's how it was. Or maybe the sisters just didn't want it, would have been reminded of Walter III every time a lease check came, I don't know. These are all people you can't ask anymore.

So, the section by the school that had been quartered already, how it worked was Arthur King ran the east two quarters of it—his and his dead brother's—and Rooster bought the front quarter, the one right on the corner by the church, from one of the sisters' families. The quarter-section above that, though, that sister's kids kept it, leased it out in strips. It changed hands almost every year. You never knew for sure who was working it.

And all that, that's the easy part of it.

Arthur King, of course, had the four kids too, just like his dad. All boys this time, three of them set to inherit, the fourth one dead. The dead one's name: Sterling. Sterling King, yeah. The one Arthur had been coddling his whole life, the golden boy, the oldest, the one who never got in trouble, did everything right, the apple of everybody's eye, all that.

The one who, in 1968, in the parking lot of a bar in Odessa at two in the morning, cocked a lever action .44-40 into his mouth and pulled the trigger, leaving a widow and two kids behind.

That rear window shattering into the night behind him, it was loud enough that Arthur King's wife, Sterling's mom, heard it forty miles away, sat straight up in her bed, and then started—it's the only way to say it—folding back into herself.

I only remember her as a tiny woman in her big chair, her hands shaky and terrifying, her lips the same color as her face.

But the land.

Everything in West Texas, it always comes back to the land.

Just as his father had before him, Arthur King quietly added his dead son's quarter of that section to his own. And the rest of the quarter-sections too. Should it have gone to the ex-daughter-in-law, Sterling King's widow? By law, maybe, though there was no will, because who ever thought Sterling could really die? Arthur's argument, maybe: it was King land. And before two years were gone she was married again anyway, had a different name, one her kids took as well, so.

Nobody said anything.

That night Sterling pointed his own gun back at himself, Arthur King's land holdings doubled.

And, until that December seventeen years later, the year of the fire, he hadn't sold a single acre of it off.

Marcus Weeks was able to tell me for sure it was December because that's when the Moores bought their new house, the one I thought they'd always lived in. And, so as not to get him in trouble, lose him any business (like that's his real name), that's pretty much all he told me. But that's all I needed, too, to connect the rest of this.

Come March 1986, it wasn't one of Arthur King's John Deeres pulling a breaking plow across that particular quarter-section, it was one of Rooster's ugly red Cases. A four-wheel-drive job, the four-bottom plow set deep to turn all that land upside down.

He didn't buy the land directly from Arthur King, though. Arthur King never would have dealt with Rooster. Like the bad guy in some worse play, Rooster, he had a way about him that...I don't know. One ear was molded plastic, from some truck exploding on him before I was born, back when the gas tanks were behind the seats, and he always wore these little round black glasses that looked German somehow, and his blue and white tea jug, it was famous all through Greenwood for being the single most crusty thermos to ever wait all day in a truck or up in the cab of a tractor. Probably had third-generation fish in there, blind from the sugar he sweetened his tea with.

Not that I never drank from it, but I drank from the handlines too, remember.

There was a while the summer after I graduated that I would ride around with Rooster, listen to his stories. Be sure to be seen in that passenger seat.

That's all later, though.

Then, December 1985—and it's there in the heavy flat books of the county tax office, because nobody would tell me straight up, even Marcus Weeks, who has no stake out there anymore and's already three marriages away from Greenwood—what was happening was Arthur King, for once, was selling some of his own land. *Irrigated* land.

Worse, who he was selling it to: Martin Ledbetter. Old Man Marty's son, not even pretending to farm anymore, now that his dad was gone.

Martin Ledbetter, Sheryl Ledbetter's dad.

I'm not sure about property prices back then—now, even—but my guess is that Arthur King named his own price here, pretty much.

Trick was, Martin Ledbetter wouldn't have been buying land to *farm*. He wore slacks, had creases in the arms of his shirts, a tan from the golf course. No, what Martin Ledbetter was buying was Rob King. And who he was paying, through Arthur King—because that's how the money had to go, the only way it could have gone—was Tommy Moore's dad, who had every right, every reason to press charges, to demand justice.

This is what Marcus Weeks means when he leans over the trunk of a Buick priced to move and crosses his arms at the wrist so that his hands just hang there in the heat, and tells me that that was when the Moores got that big new house that'd been for sale forever, yeah?

The reason Tommy Moore's dad didn't press charges against Rob King was that Arthur King came to see him, had a clutch of cash, a handshake to follow. A hollow apology afterwards, to make sure the handshake stuck. This is how things are done in Greenwood, Texas.

But this is also how things are done: the money was from Martin Ledbetter, who couldn't have cared less if Rob King went away for a year or two. However, if Rob King did get prosecuted, then there would be witnesses. One in particular, his youngest, his last, the only one not married. And, if she did testify in open court, how could she ever marry then?

Which is where Ms. Godfrey's story picks up.

***

Sheryl and Tommy are pretty much done up on top of the module. Laughing. They can see the school from here, even. All the little cars moving back and forth.

Tommy puts his pants on without sitting up, just stands on his heels and the back of his head, looking through his eyebrows for a moment to Sheryl, shrugging into her bra.

"Don't," she says, but doesn't turn away from him either.

Tommy pushes his hand deep into his front pocket, comes up with a crumpled pack of cigarettes, says to Sheryl "here."

He's not offering her a smoke. It's a kind of code between them, after these last two years together: when the wind's up, she'll let him use her shirt to make a calm space he can spark his lighter up in.

It's a stupid game, just an excuse to get her shirt off. But it's a wonderful game too, the best one ever.

Are they going to get married someday?

It's what you always think. What you can't help but think. What I was already thinking, holding a girl's hand at a football game.

It's not what you really want, though. What you really want, on top of a module like that, a girl billowing her shirt out so you can duck into it, get your cigarette going, is for that moment, for the two of you, to last forever. To live in the balloon.

Another part of the game, especially if Sheryl's wearing a front-clasp bra, is for Tommy to pretend he's still trying to get his cigarette going. This involves holding that first drag in, and holding it, holding it, his lungs curling in on themselves but it's worth it too, if he can reach through, undo that clasp.

Except they're usually not on top of a module when this happens.

This time, with the wind going, Ms. Godfrey's shirt doesn't fall over Tommy's head like it usually does. No, this time it lifts up, drifts cleanly off the module, floats for ten feet, twenty feet and only stops when Geoff Koenig snatches it from the air, holds it up like a prize he's won, the rest of the basketball team whooping and hollering.

Tommy Moore stands from the blue tarp, says it: "Fidel's going to bust your asses, you know?"

"Not if somebody doesn't tell," one of the three T's calls back, his hands on his knees so he can breathe, his eyes locked on the chance of Ms. Godrey showing something. Of Sheryl Ledbetter letting a hand slip.

She slides to the other side of the tarp, away from leering eyes. Hands at her throat, arms straight down, only making it all better.

Marcus Weeks—this seems like him—nabs the shirt from Geoff Koenig, holds it to his face, breathes in deep, then it's a game, them passing the shirt back and forth, Sheryl yelling down to them, one of the three T's finally stopping, holding it up but taking it back at the last moment.

"Smoke?" he says up to the top of the module.

"*Tommy,*" Sheryl says, her eyes hot, this game so over.

But Tommy Moore's laughing, can't help it. Doesn't know whose side he's on here anymore.

He holds the empty pack up, crumples it, lets it fall, blow away.

"Well then," whichever T has the shirt says, and the basketball players swirl around again through the stalks with their captured flag of a shirt, are running back to school, their footfalls so quiet, like they weren't even there.

The next part you already know: Tommy Moore rolling to look over the edge of the module, expecting Marcus or Geoff to be there with the shirt, but instead, his last cigarette dangling from his lip so cool, he gets dragged down into a world of hurt, won't be physically able to smile again for months, will have to go through nicotine withdrawal with an IV spiked into him.

And does he remember what happened next?

What had to have happened.

Arthur King rumbling up beside Rob King's truck, Pete Manson's door already opened. Pete Manson getting pushed away at first, falling back into Arthur King, then both of them looking up to the module, to the apparition there: one of the Ledbetter girls, the last one, standing there in the daylight in her bra—she had to look topless at first, as white as she is—but wholly unaware of it. Just screaming and screaming for Rob King to stop.

Seeing her up there like that, neither Pete Manson nor Arthur King could have had a single thing to say.

Just—just wrench Rob King away from the kid, try to hold him down for Chrissake, and somehow there's already sirens. Everybody can smell the smoke by now.

And then, and this makes all the difference, Pete Manson looking up to Sheryl Ledbetter there on the module, and holding his hand out flat before him, telling her lower, lower, lie down. Hide.

Chapter Four

The only snapshot left of Walter King III, the only I've ever seen anyway, is this skinny kid by the tack shed at the King Place. It wasn't new even then, that shed, was already leaning over, had been built with some flaw right from the beginning.

In the square little picture—one of his sisters holding the camera?—he's standing by the shed, his arms crossed, his smile nearly as wide as his face.

His sister's probably smiling too, having a hard time keeping Walter III still, or getting his shakiness to match up with the camera's, anyway. I have to guess this is the one picture from the roll that came out like they wanted. And how long would they have had to wait for it, to see? Like we all used to, I'm sure they had to go to the Stanton drugstore to drop the film off, then wait a week, two weeks. Until the film was ready *and* they had a reason to be in Stanton.

It was worth it, though.

What they'd done, what took some time doing, was they'd pulled an old pair of boots down from somewhere, then—roofing nails would be best, but I'd guess they stacked washers—they, or probably Walter III, nailed that pair of boots to a wide plank. Next they somehow (you can't tell from the picture) anchored that plank so that it canted away from the tack shed.

So, then—this is the joke—Walter III could step into those boots, wave his arms around for balance, and, at some perfect moment, cross his arms and hold it, let his sister take this impossible snapshot: him leaning away from the shed at the same angle the shed's leaning away from him.

It makes you want to turn the picture one way, then another.

His smile doesn't go away, either, is at the exact center.

On the back of the picture, too, in careful pencil that's almost gone, just one word, *Mouse*.

It's what everybody called Walter III.

The only other place I can find any photograph of him, it's his obituary. He's not smiling as big in it, and his hair's been buzzed off, but still, it's him.

Growing up, all I ever knew about him was that he died in World War II. That he was a legitimate hero, enough that Walter Jr. got his medals in the mail, then a handshake at the door, a thank you that was supposed to be from the whole country.

Did Walter Jr. stand there on the porch for half an hour after that black car was gone, his cheeks sucked in, just staring, until his wife came out, led him back into the house?

I think so, yes.

But that's not where it ends.

***

December 1985. Three days after Christmas. The basketball tournament down in Iraan that afternoon and, if Greenwood wins, that night as well. It's what offseason's been all about: conditioning. One game at two, another at eight that you're just as ready for.

In the locker room, everybody packing their gym bags and passing them to the right so somebody else can check, make sure there's shoes, socks, jocks—it's a drill by now, and for good reason—Coach Harrison sits down and looks from player to player, from face to face. And to the one missing, the one the team has already been to see again that morning.

Tommy Moore had held his hand up from his bed and each of them—the three T's, Geoff Koenig, Marcus Weeks, Dwayne Roberts—touched their palm to him lightly, not sure how breakable he still might be.

None of them had said anything about Ms. Godfrey. Maybe to their parents, but Ms. Godfrey was a Ledbetter then, and if Tommy wasn't giving her away, then no way any of them would. And, anyway, it hadn't been her fault in the first place, right?

But, the basketball team.

Now that Steve Grimes was mostly cleared, everybody was looking back to them. And Coach knew it, had called all six of the players who hadn't been wearing pads that morning into his office. Two of them had come out blinking away tears, but none of them said anything about Ms. Godfrey, and all of them swore that all they did was run out there, tell Tommy Moore to go to hell, then lean west, come back to the school one row at a time.

On the back of each of their left shoes, in careful electric tape, is the letter T. On the heel of the right, an M wide enough to cup the heel.

Coach has seen it but isn't making them peel it off.

For a long time he just sits there, staring at the skating-rink smooth concrete. The preacher at the front of his congregation, listening for a voice only he can hear. Waiting for it to be done. Trying to get it into human words.

"We didn't do it," he says at last.

General agreement.

"And Tommy, he didn't do it either."

More agreement.

"And it's not our job to figure out who did, right?"

No, it's not.

"What is our job?"

This is where you squint.

Finally somebody says it: "Play basketball, sir."

Coach: "Excuse me?"

Louder: "Play basketball, sir!"

He smiles without really smiling, a trick only coaches ever learn, then nods. Then shakes his head no.

"Play basketball?" he says, standing. "*Play* basketball?"

Little to no eye contact now.

Usually his sermons are about defense, about fouls, about what the team should remember about Crane or Colorado City from last year, since most of their players are returning as well.

"That's our job, gentlemen? To just go out there, say we *played*?"

A few smiles now. On accident.

"We're supposed to win, sir."

"What?"

"Win, sir. We're supposed to go out there and *win* the basketball game."

Again, Coach looking from face to face. Not asking for it back at him louder this time, because quiet's louder now.

"For the one of us who can't be here," he adds, taking somebody's shoulder in his hand, shaking that whole player gently, fatherly. "For the one—"

And here he doesn't finish.

It may as well be screaming into a bullhorn. Everybody blinking away the stuff rising in them. Everybody knowing they're going to win, that they have to win, that's all there is this time. That if they win, then everybody will know they were out running the whole time, not cadging smokes from Tommy Moore. Not running from module to module, grinding cherries into those crumbly white walls, even though the new rumor is that there had been a cigarette butt at each module, that the Sheriff's office still has those butts in some evidence locker like Cinderella's shoe.

Never mind that the fires had already been burning for eight hours by the time they were lacing their shoes that morning in the locker room.

Everybody knows that. But they also can't imagine who else could have been out there. Maybe the fire department's wrong about the time. Cotton's finicky, not something you can understand in a lab. And, anyway, none of the suspicious trucks have turned up. It has to be somebody. Or a team of somebodies.

But if they can play hard enough, come back with the medal, well. There's no better way to get in the good graces of a West Texas community.

So they check each other's bags, and the manager pulls the clean jerseys from the blue box, calls out numbers each player responds to, and then they're sitting on the bus at eighty-thirty in the morning. Slapping each other on the back, most of them plugged into Walkmans, making promises to themselves, trading the rest of their lives for one perfect shot, if that's what it takes for Tommy.

It's still Christmas break, so the parking lot's empty, the whole school's empty.

And the ankles traded for Tommy Moore in this tournament, the knees wrenched diving after a ball he would have dove for, the noses bloodied in his honor: none. Not a one.

But that's not to say that nobody gets hurt here.

***

One of the stories my dad used to tell me about basketball was a tournament he played in high school. Stanton was up against one of the even smaller schools, the ones that don't exist anymore, that, driving out on some narrow, unmaintained road, you can still stumble across like the ruins of some unrecorded civilization. The gym a Quonset skirted in brick, its metal doors chained shut, that floor space not reclaimed by senior citizens because the roof's not stable enough anymore.

I used to find them all the time, for hundreds of miles in any direction I went.

This game my dad would tell me about, it was one of those small gyms, probably one of the ones I saw, even, where the walls of the place were—except for one side, where the shallow stands were—almost right at the base- and sidelines. So you didn't dive out of bounds to save the ball like you can now with the extra room.

Except for once, that is, this particular game. A player from the other team, a player who'd spent hours and hours in that gym, had grown up in it, likely. Knew every dead spot, all the angles.

What happened was the ball was careening down for the baseline, and, because there was no air conditioning for a place that large, and it was night anyway, the single doors at both ends were chocked open.

What he did, then, what he knew to do, had probably done a hundred times in practice, was plant a foot at the baseline and jump, reaching for the ball, all his momentum aimed to carry him through that open door. An instant later the ball would come slinging back and the crowd would erupt. The best magic trick ever. How heroes are made.

The only difference—and I'm not even sure I'm not being lied to here—the only difference this time was that this player wasn't moving at practice speed but at game speed, where things count.

He planted like usual, jumped, got his palm on the ball just as it was slipping out the door, but he was moving too fast, went too high, high enough that his face connected with the top of the door frame, acted as a hinge for the rest of him, folding out into the night.

No ball came back. No player.

By the time everybody followed, he was just laid out, there was nothing they could do. Breathing, but bleeding chunky gouts from the mouth with each breath.

It was only after they'd carried him away to somebody's station wagon, the two-row stands emptied, that one of the Stanton players jerked his hand back from the door frame he'd been hanging onto, to lean out, watch these strange goings-on.

The knocked-out player's two front teeth were up there, buried in the wood.

Yeah, I don't know.

I've been in those gyms, though, through the windows with the grates folded up just enough, and I can see where a story like that might have happened once somewhere—some teeth lost anyway—then got improved in the retelling, told around here like it was true. Told to me like it was gospel, the most amazing thing ever. A lesson, even, that some balls aren't worth going after.

The gym I grew up in, the old gym in what used to be the main part of Greenwood, it was a Quonset too, though with more room around it. Not enough to dive through, but enough for cheerleaders anyway, if they were careful, kind of kicked to the side. The lights took something like fifteen minutes to heat up. One time, kicked out of the school I'd been trying to go to for a couple of weeks (Midland Lee or Midland High, I tried them both), I sneaked back, lucked my way through the halls of Greenwood and hid in that gym shooting baskets in the dark until my old math teacher zeroed in on the dribbles I couldn't help—the clock always counting down from ten—just stood there in the doorway and told me, her voice not even raised, that I was wasting all my potential, that I didn't have to do this, that I could be anything, that other kids would kill to have what I had. The usual story; I'd heard it before, from Ms. Everett, from Ms. Easton, and would get it in the way Godfrey looked at me that last semester before I was supposed to have graduated. I'm not mad at her for it. When Ms. Marugg told me that, I mean, she was probably younger than I am now.

I don't know.

As to why I came back there instead of the thousand and one more places I could have gone, it has something to do with that basketball tournament after the fire, I suspect—after that morning, basketball was sacred, a holy act, you were pure just because you *played*—but it also had something to do with my uncles telling me in the fourth grade to look on the wall for their initials.

It took until the sixth grade, when the pegboard was the hot thing, but I finally found them, up high on the wall, like they'd carved them in their day.

It felt good, rubbing my fingertips over those grooves, those scars.

Because they'd been just as stupid as I was being, I mean— here was the proof—but they'd made it through somehow, got away. Maybe I would too. Maybe this was all part of it.

I was a long way from that shed I'd found, anyway. A long way from just drinking sudden aftershave.

Here I am though, right?
Because of—I don't know.
According to Ms. Godfrey, it's to write all this down, to be that player disappearing into that square of night, slinging the ball back that can save the game once and for all.
I kind of doubt it.

***

It was because Leonard was late to start the bus. It was because Geoff Koenig's mom had to drive his shoes up, pass them through the window in a folded-over paper bag that smelled like peaches. It was because Fidel made one of the three T's go back inside, *shave*. It was because Coach got a phone call just as they were all walking out. It was because the sun was shining, it was because the Reverends Green and Wood had liked the lay of this land, it was because Texas had been stolen from Mexico.

It was none of that. It was all of that.

It was the team and the coaches and the two managers watching the rows of cotton to either side of them speed up, whip past.

Instead of going straight up FM 1379 to the Garden City Highway to hook it through Rankin to Iraan, they turned *left* out of the high school parking lot and stopped at the church, Leonard looking both ways three stupid times like he always did then turning east on Cloverdale, no traffic at all, not a car or truck or witness for miles.

And maybe that was it, yeah. Instead of going across on 20, to Odessa, and because 1379 was torn up in some way up the road—Leonard still lived up toward Sprayberry, would have known—the bus was hooking it over to 137, to go south.

By this time, Rob King was home, of course, his right hand useless to control the throttle on a tractor, but he could throttle and steer with his left hand, and dump the baskets too, or run the module builder, whatever was needed, his cast the whole time wrapped in a plastic bag, his co-op hat pulled low so nobody could see his eyes, his left hand always opening and closing these days. Opening and closing.

As for the trampoline that had blown into the fence or his pump house that the wind had exploded, those weren't important yet. There was still *some* cotton to be packed into modules, anyway.

Christmas had been quiet, strained.

All the boys wore pants to the breakfast table, chewed their food thoroughly. Belinda King cried, swept away in her robe, came back ten minutes later, her cheer such a mask that the two younger boys started crying too.

Rob King stood at the window, stared down the empty rows, the brown stalks arm bones to him. All the people planted out there, reaching up for something.

He understood.

Under the tree was supposed to have been the spark plug to a three-wheeler for the boys to share, a Honda 110 he'd been talking about since school had started.

None of them had asked after it, though. Not out loud.

The skin of the trampoline caught in the fence was losing its basket weave, the fibers fraying. By dusk it was some crash-landed wraith. The biggest, deadest crow ever.

By noon he was back out in the fields, stripping alone.

Soon enough Arthur King joined him and they worked together, no words necessary after all these seasons.

In the back of *his* truck, Arthur's, wrapped under a tarp, was the Honda 110.

Rob King didn't say anything, just nodded, took it home filled with gas, and the headlight worked, and that night there were two boys with blue lips, one helmet between them, Belinda King on the porch, trying not to say anything.

Rob King probably puts his arm around her waist here.

Give them that.

Three days later, though, he's in the fields again, the boys too, with promises to be careful, to take turns. But Belinda's standing on the porch just the same. Already Jonas has got his heel caught on the knobby front of one of the rear tires, been pulled down between the fender and peg, the three-wheeler bouncing over him, his back for a moment bent like Belinda's trying hard to forget.

If she could just be out there with them, she thinks.

She'd trade a quiet cup of coffee alone at the table for her boys, yes. Any day.

But she can't hear the three-wheeler from the porch, so she steps out to the drive, to the basketball goal one of Rob's brothers welded together as a housewarming gift, never mind that the cable rusted within the month, seized in the pulley, so the rim's never been higher than seven feet six inches

It's low enough she can hook the fingers of her right hand in the bottom of the net, lean there, study the horizon for a speck of Honda red.

Instead, she finds some school-bus yellow.

It's just sitting there on Cloverdale, its nose in the ditch.

Belinda King tightens her grip on the net, pulls herself up to her toes to see better, and already her heart's hammering in her chest.

They're not supposed to cross the road.

They're not supposed—

II

Chapter Five

Mouse. Mouse King. King Mouse. K-Man. Just "King," like he was the only one, or "Walt," like his dad, Arthur King's grandfather.

I don't know what they called Walter III in the Army.

That summer I rode around with Rooster, he only ever called him Mouse.

That summer Arthur King's wife would be dead one morning on the couch when he came back in from his coffee, the television news flickering across her face.

By the time the medics got there, Arthur King would be back in the shop, hammering a sand-polished three-foot knife back to true, his plastic goggles on.

I like to think it was to keep the medics from seeing his eyes, from knowing he was human like them, but the truth is probably the same as it is for everybody who works in shops: you know somebody who caught a sliver of metal in their eye.

Get a splinter in your finger, your body'll push it out after a while. In your eye, though, with metal—what happened with my Uncle Parker was it started to rust, to send out these branches of brown. He got to it early enough, though, got to keep his eyes. He was the uncle who'd opened his closet for me one day, told me I could take any three books I wanted—

Mack Bolan, Louis L'Amour, Conan, Raymond Chandler, the paperbacks six thick in some places—then three more when I got through with those.

Four years later I'd burned through all of them, was raiding any other closet I could find.

Thank you.

But still, it was Jackson I tried to walk like, Jackson I still hold my head like. I can see it in pictures.

He wasn't around Greenwood very much anymore, was usually pulling trailers of pipe or oilfield equipment back and forth between Dallas and El Paso, but sometimes went as far east on 20 as Jackson, Mississippi.

Whatever music he listened to, I listened to.

When he'd blast through, let me ride in his truck, pull the horn—he was my secret dad, the one never on a tight enough schedule that he couldn't go back, see what that glittering thing had been in the ditch.

Until my sixth grade, anyway.

I was standing in front of the school on a Friday night, waiting for the purple bus to come over from Stanton like a UFO. Waiting for Herb to unfold that magic door, ferry us to the skating rink for Van Halen and Ms. Pac-Man and hobo races and limbo and quarter refills at the fountain, dark corners and slow dances and fights in the bathroom, lockers by girls we were in love with. Our names said slow over the big speakers in a way I'll never forget. It was the whole gang of us, the usual suspects, and then there was this blue-striped cab-over weaving into the parking lot too fast, swinging wide but close enough that we shielded our eyes from the gravel.

Uncle Jackson. He'd changed rigs.

I walked over, unsure, leading the pack.

Soon enough the door opened and he half-fell, half-climbed down, leaving dark handprints on the chrome grab bar, something like steam rising from every part of him. Or smoke. Like he'd been in a whole other world, was just climbing back up to this one. For me.

The way he was breathing, too, it was wrong, and it was almost dark already, and I was about to cry, I knew, even though I was twelve and all my friends were there.

But then he smiled, his teeth the only thing on him that could reflect light.

I never understood quite what, but the tank he'd just dropped off out on the Rankin Highway, it had hot oil in it, or oil that had got hot in the sun maybe, or out on the interstate, and some seal or line had burst, spilling that oil all over him, cap to boot laces. He was burned—burning—but not bad enough that he couldn't still smile, show us not to be afraid.

The reason he was there, though.

This is the part I hate.

He knelt, the rocks and broken glass sticking to the knee of his jeans in a way that made me pull my lips away from my teeth.

"I need—need you to drive," he told me, there in front of everybody, and then swallowed so that I could see the effort it was taking him to control his voice here.

I opened my mouth, didn't have any sound.

He'd let me do it before, him working the complicated gears, the steering wheel like a huge bowl I could lean too far over, fall down into, but this, this was different.

"Drive," he said, like I wasn't getting it. Like I didn't understand the urgency. What this hot oil was doing to him. How hard it was to even be standing still.

It was the closest he'd ever come to raising his voice to me.

"I—I can't," I told him.

My excuse that night at the skating rink would be that I didn't want to go to jail for not having a license, and I'd try to say it like that was the only thing I could have done. Like I knew enough not to want to go to jail. Like I didn't need that kind of hassle, not on a Friday night, when the cops could keep me all the way until Monday if they wanted.

It's dark at the skating rink, too. Whoever you're couple-skating with, she usually can't see your face.

I didn't get in any fights that night. Probably even won the limbo again, I don't know. It was always mine for the taking. My friend Bryan—the one who lived by where Prairie Lee used to be—drank all the vinegar out of the gallon pickle jar and then threw up in the parking lot, had to beg his way back in, but that was nothing new.

Hours before that, though. It was skating around and around in my head, like maybe if I looked close enough at the rail there would be a hand to pull me back, give me another chance. Let me do it again, right this time.

But it only happens once in your life, a thing like this.

In the parking lot, dusk all around us, Jackson cocks his head over, maybe not sure I'd really said that, that I didn't want to *drive*, then looks to the rest of the sixth graders behind me. Not for someone else to drive, but like seeing them for the first time.

"Just down to your dad's, man," he says, reaching for me, his arm almost straight. "C'mon, dude."

I flinch back. Have my favorite shirt on.

"No," I tell him, taking another step away, and he stays there on one knee for maybe ten more seconds, just staring at me, then nods, says it in a way that there isn't any disappointment in his voice, "Cool, man," and climbs back up, locks his left leg against the clutch, and, and—

And the first novel I ever sketched out, that years later became my first novel except all different, the key moment is when this underage kid's driving a cab-over rig by himself, trying to make it to these ancestral carnival grounds but he's already late, so late.

Then, because the world's against him, has been the whole time, the bridge he's about to duck under—I'd seen *Terminator 2* by then—it collapses. But he keeps on driving, shears the top off his rig, then sits up, lines that big steering wheel back into place and reaches down for a taller gear, twin plumes of black smoke chugging up behind him.

I don' t know.

So, Parker, yeah, thanks, seriously and forever, and Jackson, man: you tried. The next time I saw you, it was at your mom's funeral. Your blue rig was parked out on Cloverdale, past all the other cars. I stared and stared at it.

***

And there's Rooster. Rooster Jones. Jones being the real last name for once. But there's a lot of us, don't worry. And I wasn't going by Jones that summer after graduation anyway, had been through so many names already that it might as well have been witness protection.

Like he'd been waiting my whole life, too, like I should know this before he pulled up onto the road, as it might decide whether I went down it with him, he just told me up front why Arthur King didn't prefer his company.

It was Mouse.

Rooster and Mouse had been in the same company in the Army.

Before, the story I'd been able to put together involved Mouse staying behind to provide cover while the rest of his troop made it back to the trenches. Or that's the one I'd been telling myself. Probably I got it from the movies. All I had to do was put that World War II uniform onto that kid leaning away from the tack shed, take it from there.

As for why Arthur King didn't enlist, why his brother was there instead of him, I suspect it had to with Walter Jr. needing to keep at least one of them there to plow the fields, tend the crop. At least one.

How do you pick, though?

Who has to stand on top of that cellar door, hold onto the cable?

My guess: Mouse made the decision himself. Going by the stories I've heard about him, all cleaned up by time and telling, not only would he have never let it be anybody *but* him, but trumpets would have been sounding in the background, a lion roaring in the distance. Anyway, by that time, Arthur was already married, had a kid on the way, while Mouse was just Mouse. Spent so much time on the tractor that he probably didn't even need a bed.

And Walter Jr. couldn't have said no, either. Maybe the war would be good for Mouse, get him on the family track, show him what's important. Not that he wasn't an excellent hand, not that anybody in the county disliked him, but if he was going to take over the whole operation, he was going to need a proper home to come back to at night, right? To remind him why he was working so hard.

So, yeah, he signed up, actually got sent to the front lines instead of some safe post, and never came back. The usual tragedy. This is how you make a saint.

Except for Rooster Jones.

Even in 1945, I have to imagine he had about the same effect on people as he would forty-five years later, when I was riding around with him. And as for *his* home life, I have no idea. His wife was somebody he joked about every chance he got—Wanda, I think—but I never saw her step out of the house. And his three kids, all boys, were from my dad's generation, one in jail for a good stretch, one looking to retire from the Army after his twenty, the other supposedly still around somewhere, just in some slightly different sphere of West Texas than I ever moved in.

1990 doesn't matter here, though. Just World War II. What really happened to Mouse.

According to Rooster, the one time Arthur King ever graced his porch was when he had a paper for Rooster to sign.

It wasn't quite a legal document, but it was phrased like an affidavit, anyway. For the *Midland Reporter-Telegram*. Because Rooster hadn't been returning any of their letters, and never answered his phone.

This is Titans meeting on that porch.

Arthur stone-faced with jealousy, with resentment, because it wasn't him who got to see Mouse go down, wasn't him who got to nod goodbye, to pack everything into that nod: that they understood what he was doing, that it wouldn't be forgotten. That they were all going to live with more purpose now, just in honor, in thanks.

I can kind of see Rooster on that porch, too, shrugging his shoulders like he'd just thought of a joke, his round little sunglasses still on even though it's almost dark, his whole manner saying that he was well aware what Greenwood thought of him: that he had got there seventy years too late. That the money he was buying their land up with, it wasn't honest money.

"They just want to know that's how it happened," Arthur King says here, to Rooster, holding the document between them. "It's for the bicentennial write-up."

Of course there would only ever be the obituary, that one PFC photograph.

This is the why of that.

Rooster laughs here, rubs his nose with the back of his always-buttoned sleeve—his burn-scarred arms still sensitive to the sun—and shakes his head no, Artie. No.

Some pretty serious silence here. Mrs. Jones maybe at the window, holding her breath. A jackrabbit out grubbing up pink careless weed roots but stopped now, its lanky ears cocked over.

"Why?" Arthur King says. "Can you tell me that, at least?"

A smile from Rooster. A simpering, simpering smile, like the mischievous dog in a cartoon.

"This is probably something for Junior to be relating, think?" Rooster says then.

"You were there," Arthur King says.

"That's what I'm saying," Rooster says back, shrugging that, more than anybody, he wishes he hadn't been.

How long Arthur King stands there after this, I don't know. But they don't say anything else, don't nod bye. At some point one of them finally just turns away, goes either to his truck or his front door, and in this way it's over, and the article never gets into print.

It's still floating around, though.

Forty-five years later, Rooster screws the cap off his rancid thermos and gives it to me, tells me what Arthur didn't ask—what Arthur didn't have to ask—tells me it like it's my inheritance, but first asks me what I know.

"He stayed back," I say, trying to shrug it real, "he stayed back, held the Germans off, so the rest of you…you know."

It feels so strange to even be saying it, at eighteen. Saying it out loud. And I realize I never have. How thin it is, this story. How flimsy. "The Germans." I didn't even know what that meant, back then. Shouldn't even be allowed to say it at all.

Rooster smiles, splashes a few swallows of his milky tea into the cap, passes it over to me.

I swirl it around to try to get the sediment or backwash to be harder to see, anyway, then drink it down in two shut-eyed gulps.

Rooster nods, fills it again and drinks it off, holding it in his mouth a bit before swallowing, like getting all the taste out. Or waiting for it to warm down enough for his throat. Then he screws the cap back on and taps the thermos into place between us.

"Mouse," he says, not looking at his cotton so much anymore. "This would be a different countryside now, you know?"

I don't, but nod anyway.

One old guy could have made everything different?

Or, one old guy did, I guess. Has.

"Ever wonder why Mouse didn't leave any little Mouslings behind?" Rooster says, scurrying his fingers up the face of the dash.

"He died," I say back. It's obvious.

Rooster pinches some chewing tobacco up, packs it in. Lets the juices build until I think I might have to scream.

Where we are is back by the Phillips place, the pasture between the fields always a haunted place for me. Most of the owls and snakes I killed, I hid them there. According to Jackson, he and Parker used to think it was an Indian burial ground. Before the mesquite—and maybe this is a story he got second-hand, as the mesquite there are *trees*—the pasture was supposed to have been lumpy, back when. Evenly lumpy, in rows.

Because that's how Indians buried their dead, yeah.

But who knows.

It wasn't always Indians burying the Indians, either.

The Phillips place was always kind of special to me, anyway. The only place I ever saw a mountain lion track. Just a line of them, angling towards Cloverdale through the soft dirt. Huge pads, no claws. I was moving pipe that morning. Everybody else always had stories about seeing them, just at the edge of their headlights. About pulling up to a draw and jumping a big one, one that moves like smoke from a yellow smoke bomb. About the guy at the trailer park back by the water station who'd hit a black panther one night after the bar and has it in his chest freezer now.

All I ever got were the tracks, though, so I had to make the cat up myself, then be afraid to bend over for the pipe, because I'd made it up too good.

Like I say, though, I wasn't writing then, wouldn't even be considering that until my *other* uncle got burned. Parker, eighty percent of his body third-degree.

This time I went.

The campus police came and got me from world lit, even.

If I hadn't reached back for my backpack, too, I wouldn't be here right now. In that backpack was the spiral I was supposed to have been taking notes in.

The reason the campus police got me was that I was the only family Parker had in Lubbock, where he'd been flown to the burn unit. The only reason they got me was because he wasn't supposed to live.

Of course I couldn't go back, see him, so just sat there at the doors, with this other family.

What had happened to them was—this was Halloween too, like with Pete Manson's little brother—this dad, a guy about six-and-a-half feet tall, a biker like everybody in the waiting room, he'd been out trick-or-treating with his six-year-old. In the car. Only, they didn't drive it very much, so the tires had got weathered. Just a few houses in, not even half a bag of candy collected, the driver's side rear popped. Not a blowout or anything, just a flat. This was out on the Slaton Highway, I think (my freshman year, every Lubbock road I didn't know was the Slaton Highway). So this guy, this dad, he's out there changing the tire, and some repeat offender weaves by, slams right into him, drags him two hundred feet down the road, leaves him all over the asphalt. The kid just sitting there in his mask.

And that should have been it, yeah. People don't live through that.

But this guy was, somehow.

He was in the ICU slot closest to the door, all his family and friends bunched up around it. What kept happening was that he was waking up, ripping all the cords and hoses and lines from his face and body, fighting the doctors so he could get off that bed. The only thing he was saying was his son's name. His son there once, in the remains of his five-dollar costume, his candy bag a plastic pumpkin with a delicate black chinstrap for a handle.

Because I had to be looking somewhere, not at him, I opened my spiral, tried to go anywhere else. By the time I came back, the dad had died.

Parker was supposed to too, but didn't.

The other day, on my birthday, he called me, even. I had no clue he had my number. Where he lives now is an apartment in Dallas that I've never been to. Since the accident, he doesn't read anymore, says he can't stay focused that long.

What I always want to ask him is about the graves, though. The Phillips place. If Jackson and him ever just dug out there one day. What they could have found if they had.

Skeletons of all of us, I'd guess. Hiding, waiting. Trying to pull the dirt back over.

***

According to Rooster, what Mouse did in World War II, it didn't have anything to do with medals. But it made a kind of sense, too.

Junior had a certain sickness, was the thing.

The kind that only ever fixes on one of the kids. The one he named after himself.

Of course Mouse went to war instead of his brothers. It's what he'd already been doing his whole life, every seventh or eighth night when the boots came down the hall. When he was lying in bed, staring at the ceiling, praying it wouldn't be tonight. That he'd worked hard enough already.

And Arthur King had to have known. To have remembered. To have forgotten ten thousand times but then had it rise back up a hundred more. For the sisters too, I'd guess, but they could marry out. Try to shake these childhoods off, be somebody else. Never come back, even for Christmases, even for all the funerals. Never mind the land. Never mind any of it.

So, the story Rooster tells is that their company, fourteen of them that day, were moving through light cover, trying to make it back to the trucks. But it was the middle of the day. And there wasn't some whole battalion dogging their every step, about to roll over them. Eventually, sure, but not right then.

What there was was a single soldier out there, separated from his unit. A single soldier with a single rifle.

One scared guy, herding Rooster and Mouse's whole company.

"Medals," Rooster says, then laughs a sick little laugh.

And I know this was 1945, but I don't know France from Italy from any other World War II battlefield. I know they were over there, somewhere. In dry grass, not snow. And that—this an embellishment from the obituary, probably Walter Jr.'s doing, because he did know enough people—Mouse's "valorous" action resulted in twelve soldiers making it back to their families.

Twelve, not thirteen. Which is what you get when you take one Mouse away from fourteen soldiers.

I mention this to Rooster. Like I'm the new Arthur King, trying to poke holes in the story.

"Good eye," Rooster says, leaning out the window to trail a line of spit that'll only make the ground after following the swelled contour of his door. A streak of rust already starting there, under the stain.

"Garrison," he says, that thirteenth soldier. Garrison something, he doesn't recall. What he had working against him, anyway, it was his height.

When they all stood up to get across a fence, Garrison's neck exploded. It was supposed to be his head, Rooster was pretty sure, but the neck would get the job done, sure.

Garrison fell over, dead. No details there.

This is when what the *Midland Reporter-Telegram* wanted to call heroics started.

Mouse didn't say any of the *go on without me* stuff, had no last messages to pass on to anyone back home.

Instead, according to Rooster—all of them were facedown in the sharp grass, all their training gone—what happened was that one moment Mouse was lying there with the rest of them, but then his eyes changed, sort of. His face going calm. Not his whole life catching up with him, burying him, and not the future opening up before him either, too haunted. No, what Mouse felt, it has to be the same thing I felt one bad night in Austin, trying to merge onto a fast street deep in the morning: that if I just make one mistake here, one understandable bad judgment, the kind people make hundreds of times each day all over the world, then nothing will matter anymore. It's the most vague way to say it, I know, but it's not about ducking obligations, not about worries or responsibilities. It's about stepping outside the cycle. Going somewhere else. Maybe nowhere.

So, me, yeah, I pulled out into that road, my muscles tense for what I knew was coming, but then all the cars screaming past, a wall of them, fell in line around me somehow, carried me along. Two miles later, my hand shaking, I put my seatbelt on.

Not Mouse.

When he saw this way he could go, what could happen here if he let it, he just flicked his eyes to Rooster once, not even in farewell, more just acknowledging that Rooster was there. He stood, Mouse. Turned to face the direction Garrison had been shot from.

And then he walked into it, even after that other soldier missed once, twice, four times, finally tugging at Mouse's trench-colored pants leg.

Mouse didn't even look down, just stood there. His arms not out dramatic and sacrificial—he was a lanky farm boy from West Texas—his cheeks dry, but still, if he just would have flinched, maybe. Regretted this though it was too late. Anything.

This war had been coming for him a long time already, though.

It's not easy being the one Daddy loved most.

And here comes the animated part of this, the cartoon: a highly detailed, nearly lovable German or Italian slug splashing through Mouse and curving up after that, losing itself in the sky for nearly half a century, finally coming back down halfway around the world.

December 1985, to be precise.

Three days after Christmas.

***

As for where exactly it happened, that's the thing: none of them could say. None of the players, anyway.

Anywhere between where they pulled up out of the parking lot and where Leonard finally stalled in the ditch, maybe a half mile later.

It made all the difference, too, where it had happened.

According to Trevor Watkins—the third T in the yearbook photo—he was rewinding his Quiet Riot to "Slick Black Cadillac" at the time. So he could hear, even past his headphones, but was mostly just concentrating on those two little sprocketed wheels, one pulling the other, one turning slow, the other furious. He was watching, his finger cocked on Stop, because this player, his brother's, ate about every third tape, and this Quiet Riot was Amber Outlaw's.

So, he could have heard it, maybe did, even, but it didn't register.

He does remember Geoff Koenig standing, and stilt-arming it back through the seats, probably to trade tapes with somebody, or to dump the paper bag out the trash window—the one furthest from Leonard—get the smell of peaches gone.

And he guesses, yeah, that Geoff Koenig did sit down. But maybe that's where he'd been going the whole time. Nobody told him there was going to be a test, right?

So, mark him off the witness list.

Marcus Weeks too. At first he claimed to have seen it all, but then Tad's story (these were the *cops*) was that he'd smuggled a certain kind of magazine onboard—like the music, to get ready for the game—and that Marcus and him had been nine seats back, directly behind Coach very much on purpose. Studying.

Marcus claimed that didn't mean he couldn't have looked up, but he didn't push it.

And as for why Coach or Leonard didn't hear it, they were at the front of the bus, where the floor's thin, the engine right there under you, and getting up to speed after the turn onto Cloverdale, it was the kind of loud you needed ear protection for.

Leonard had eyes, though, and mirrors, and was used to watching for mischief, but he didn't want Geoff Koenig to get benched just for trading seats, either, so he pretended to be concerned with making the next gear. With saying to Coach, "So that was them on the horn, yeah?"

Coach, looking away, his thumbnail finding his teeth.

Them: the college scouts already keeping a sheet on Tommy Moore. Scouts just coming back from break, just getting word that they could cancel this trip, maybe.

Does Coach Harrison look out the window here as they pass the place in Rooster's field where it happened?

If he did, he doesn't remember, has no story to fill in between leaving the parking lot and tilting into the ditch.

Even then, he thought it was maybe something with the engine. Looked ahead for cows in the road, their hotwire grounded out. Another bus needing help. Fire trucks again.

The road was empty.

"Sir," Leonard says, his eyes deep in the segmented mirror.

It's Geoff Koenig on the edge of an unoccupied seat about halfway back, his head bobbed down. Blood.

Coach Harrison stands, and by pure luck—he missed Vietnam, never had to get those terrible instincts—sees the shatter point in the side window just about even with Geoff Koenig, and says it in the voice he doesn't even use for regionals, *"Down,"* so that when Belinda King gets there, her mouth saying it even if she isn't—*thank you thank you thank you*—at first she thinks the bus is empty, steps up through the open door like a woman in an urban legend.

All there is is one boy, Lydia's son, with the big feet. Just sitting there. Bleeding.

He looks up to her and her lips are still whispering *thank you*, and she hates herself more than a little, turns her head down, to the flicker of motion beside her.

Leonard, who Rob King has stories about. Hiding between two of the seats.

Roger Harrison crouched in the next, his scalp shiny and wet through his flattop.

"Down," he whispers to her, mostly with his eyebrows, but she doesn't. Just looks around, immediately sees—there are no heads in the way now—what the Sheriff's office will draw yarn through and photograph from every possible angle: a bullet hole in one pane of glass on the driver's side of the bus, and a bullet hole in another pane as well.

"Mrs. King," Geoff Koenig says then, his voice too chipper, too polite, then shakes his head no, that he doesn't understand what's happening here. But she is a mom. It doesn't matter how tall he is anymore.

As for what he would eventually say, he wasn't going back to the trash window, and he wasn't going back for a tape or to look at the magazine or for a different seat even, though that's part of it, he guesses. It's that in the paper bag, wrapped in foil so it wouldn't get dirty from the shoes, had been a peach, for luck. And there was no eating on the bus, strict rule number one.

He'd had to hide the peach in his shorts, even, when everybody smelled it. But the foil had kept it all right, and anyway, it was his shorts, right?

He couldn't *not* eat it now, after being scratched from that foil.

Not up front with Coach, though.

So he stands, almost loses his balance, the peach rolled in his sock now, but manages to make it back two rows, three, and won't be able to remember for the Sheriff's office where they were on the road exactly when he had to sit down. When he just found himself sitting.

It was like he'd fallen, but, too—the peach. Shit.

His mom, all our moms, had told us stories about being girls in the late summer. The boys off at the stock tanks if they were young enough, out in the fields if they were that old, the girls left to play all day at the house, finally getting shooed out the front door.

It didn't matter. Everybody had a peach tree or two growing. And nothing's better on a hot afternoon. You don't even have to clean them or anything.

Once in all the girls' lives, once that they'll tell over and over, a defining afternoon, is the time one of those huge black and orange Mexican wasps that love the peaches came for them, and got them. On the back of the arm, the side, a calf, once was all it took to force this story this deep into them. And how it hurt, how they screamed, how their dads took five-gallon buckets of diesel rags out later that night and lit them, to smoke all the wasps away from their little girls. The best smell ever, why most of them grew up to marry farmers, probably: coming home from all day on the tractor, they smell like safety.

According to Geoff Koenig, anyway, at first he thought it was a Mexican wasp, sluggish in the bag, crawling out half-blind, tearing into the first thing it saw.

Except, from his shoulder, his arm—wasp bites don't bleed, do they? Even Mexican wasps, however big they are, however mad.

And where was it now?

That's probably why he sat down. To fan off the next attack.

There was just that one bullet, though. One cartoon of a .22 slug, somehow not breaking up after one window. Having enough left to cut through him, enough left after *that* to make it out the other side. A one-in-a-thousand shot. One-in-a-hundred-thousand.

For three days after this the ditches will be taped off, three metal detectors going at once. And when that doesn't work, every kind of magnet. And when the magnets just get pull tabs and beer caps, lug nuts and sheared-off bolts, there'll be grown men crawling through the grass finger by finger, then shoveling the dirt up into wheelbarrows, because somebody's said you could probably pan lead out, right?

But they don't even know if they're in the right part of the road.

It could have happened right by the school's the thing, when the bus was still on 1379, already whining down for the stop sign. Nearly an eighth of a mile of ditch to find one twisted slug in. Shattered glass all up and down it, from bottles and windshields and everything else; the church was the center of Greenwood, had been for nearly a hundred years. All manner of things had found their way out the car window on the way to Sunday school. Or even other ways.

One of my clearest memories is this Torino we had with a rusted-out floorboard. Way before seatbelts. I'm in the front floorboard, notice my mom's shiny hand. She passes her wedding ring down to me, the one from my dad's great-grandmother. She tells me to be careful, and maybe two miles later, watching the asphalt blur past not fourteen inches under me through a rusted-through hole, I hold the ring there sideways, let it go.

It doesn't make a sound, is just gone, forever. If any of the men searching the ditch for that slug found it those last few days of 1985, too, then they palmed it, kept looking.

Along with the slug?

Exactly.

***

If one of the things going on here's going to be Michael Graham's list that goes for all of us—Things the Wind's Taken Away, almost the title of this, along with The Evil Good Men Do and Where the Truth Lies—then another has to be Things That Have Turned up in the Ditch.

Cassette tapes I've spent hours respooling, just because I thought there was going to be a secret message there for me. Caps I snuck into the dishwasher when we had one, because the patch on them was so cool, the brim already broke in right. A bumpy Procter & Gamble coin that had to be from the Devil's change purse, a coin I saved for a long time all the same, to look at in secret. Pot plants growing tall and proud. Wheel wells I used to hoard, sure they were going to be the perfect thing someday, not just the mosquito hatcheries they already were. Goats I chased down on three-wheelers for a vacationing neighbor, chased down with my dad, each of us laughing so hard we could hardly drive. Once, over about a quarter mile, Polaroids of a girl in less and less clothes each time the flashbulb popped. She's skinny, not smiling. Red around the eyes.

We burned those.

Never a body, though. But I always looked, always knew it was going to happen. Once at two in the morning there was a dog just standing there waiting for me to pass, a thing in its mouth I would swear to anybody was a human hand and forearm. By the time I went back the dog was gone. Another morning, alone, the night over, a just-dead mule deer doe, a pale animal feeding on it that I still can't explain, an animal that tracked me as I passed, an animal that had this long tail not made for the burrs of West Texas. And coyotes, always watching. Just out there with a grin, a glint in their eyes, like they know something but are keeping it to themselves.

And sometimes what's in the ditch, it steps up onto the road. Just three months ago, in a store I'd never been to, a town I hardly knew, there's the girl who spent our senior year in the hospital, after her little Sunbird couldn't turn fast enough to avoid a night-black Angus just standing there, unafraid. At the end of the cereal aisle she talks about Greenwood like another life we all lived. She's not wrong.

And it's not always just cows standing there either.

A friend tells me that one night he's driving home. Too late, going too fast. Not paying enough attention to see the girl balancing on the stripe, reaching for him.

She'd been in the news then for eight days, an abduction case out of Midland. He clips her, sends her spinning into the ditch. Always the ditch.

The police don't blame him.

Another friend is four-wheeling—this is after graduation, after he's married and moved to Dallas—out at Possum Kingdom drinking by himself and climbing what he can, not rationing his gas at all, when he comes across a man hanging by his neck from a tree. The dead man's been there for days already.

My friend doesn't touch him, knows better. But he feels a kind of pride, too. Over his find. A completely understandable kind of pride. Hours later he stands by the state trooper's car watching all this commotion he's caused, and for the next few years, his girls cycling through soccer and karate and piano and cheerleading, he spends every weekend he can in more and more remote trails. Looking for dead people. Just one more.

I don't know.

He should have stayed closer to home, maybe. A guy from the grade ahead of me, who used to beat me up, one of the guys who would kick his way into your bathroom stall, arc a line of pee down between your legs, tell you to sit still now, a guy who I was sure would live forever, could weather anything, he died on a four-wheeler. Or, under it. Just puttering back to feed the pigs one night after work, his house so full of kids, each of them his perfect clone. Another girl, two years ahead of him—one year behind Ms. Godfrey—she didn't drive four-wheelers but did have this powder-blue Trans-Am, the decal on the hood sun bleached and as perfect as anything I've ever seen.

My first year driving, I would be showing off in the high school parking lot and slip into a bad series of donuts. It felt like a ride in the carnival teacups. All I could do was hold on, try to keep my head from flopping out the window. If there hadn't been gravel loose on the asphalt, I would have been rolling, not sliding. When I finally stopped, the stock rear bumper of my Ford, it was nestled into the space above the bias-ply tire but below the rear fender of a baby blue Trans-Am. Shannon—I never talked to her, even once—looking at me from under the stands, cocking her head just enough for me to know how lucky I was here.

I lied, told everybody it was on purpose, placing my bumper there, and then had my friends stand in the bed so I could ease away, not take her chrome trim with me.

This is the car she would die in two years later. Its first and last body damage. She probably still had those same old tires on it. Her house was the one we always ran behind for offseason basketball. Her sweet TA beside it, the front wheels cocked just enough sideways to be forever cool.

And maybe—she was only a year behind, would have been prime—maybe she even dated Geoff Koenig when he came back to school a hero, could pick any girl, *all* the girls.

You'd think the story of him would be this guy, forty and filling out, three marriages behind him, more kids than he can remember birthdays for. Or that he's the guy on the four-wheeler, out looking for bodies. The guy dying *under* the four-wheeler. The one hitting the missing girl, both hands tight on the wheel.

In a novel, maybe.

Today, Geoff Koenig doesn't have any kids, jokes that all those rubbers were wasted money.

Five years after high school he enlisted with the Marines for the first Gulf War. To get shot again, feel that rush of living all over? For how everybody treats you different for a while after something like that?

I don't ask him that.

He's back in Greenwood now. On the other side of 80, behind Wallace's grocery. In 1998, blind drunk, he drove his new Camaro under the rear bumper of a pipe trailer parked in the ditch on 1110, the road we all called Rabbit Run.

He lived again, somehow. Geoff Koenig had enough charm left for that, but lost most of his vision. I don't know what he sees now, just know him as a voice on a phone. He thought I was in Colorado, not sitting in my truck down at Wallace's.

What he is is another victim of that fire.

And it doesn't stop with him.

***

Stacy Monahans. She's another person I can't ask about any of this.

Not because she was two years ahead of me, and not because she was fifty miles away in Lamesa, but because ten days into 1986, the Subaru Brat she'd borrowed from her friend's boyfriend hydroplaned on 349, the road that angles from Lamesa down to Midland.

They didn't find her until the next morning.

And I say "they," but it was her father, Larry Monahans. Not out driving the roads looking for her, but sitting in a yellow seat in a turnrow, trying to rub a clean place in the glass, to see if that's a car out there or what. And then recognizing it, shaking his head, remembering what it was like to be a junior in high school like Dan—that's the Subaru kid's name, right?

So he doesn't even know until he's there, down at the shattered white side glass, trying to rub a clean place in it as well.

And I wouldn't be saying it like this if there wasn't a reason, please believe me.

I don't think he'd want me to do it any other way, though.

And as for that last name, Monahans, like the Sand Dunes, like the town at the other end of 20 out of Odessa, it's real. Real enough. His mom had married the guy with that joke of a name when Larry was fourteen, so him and his baby sister had taken it, never questioned it.

As for why his daughter was sneaking down 349 that night in a borrowed car, though, making a midnight run on just a learner's permit—everybody questioned it, and finally that afternoon, Daniel "Speedy" Gonzales, hiding at his girlfriend's, the most obvious place, licked his lips and came forward. Told it to his uncle instead of Mr. Monahans, because everybody knew the stories about Mr. Monahans, how he used to be. And so Daniel Gonzales' uncle got it to the police, what everybody in Greenwood already knew, pretty much, and would have said had Lamesa thought to ask: Stacy Monahans, summertime front desk girl for the chemical store on the north side of Lamesa, Stacy Monahans, barrel rider, Stacy Monahans, cross-country superstar, she had a boyfriend some three years older. From Greenwood.

Geoff Koenig.

What she'd borrowed Daniel Gonzales' light little Brat for was to go see him again, Geoff, to be his Florence Nightingale, his—his Sheryl Ledbetter, standing by his bed, cupping the side of his face in her hand. Making promises. Saying them over and over. Never expecting somebody to have been blowing out their handlines in *January*, making run-off that, in the cool, stood for longer than it should have.

In this whole book, she's the first person to really die all the way.

Mark that.

Chapter Six

In the background of some of the newspaper photos from the day of the shooting are the men already gathering by the bus.

Belinda King's not there anymore, her robe full of burrs from running through the CRP, but the Sheriff'll get to her soon enough.

What he'll ask, sitting in her living room, his tone mournful, like he doesn't want the answer here: There was a box of .22 long rifle shells in the stocking a week and a half ago, right?

This time there were no mystery trucks in the area, their gun racks conspicuous. No suspicious basketball players drifting through the cotton.

Just a gun out there somewhere.

That and a gold medal the head coach from Iraan had driven up in their big bus, given to Geoff Koenig's dad, his whole team in uniform, just to turn around and go home.

The medal's in the display case in the new high school now. Along with a photo of the 1985 team, taken early enough to be sure and make the yearbook. Taken early enough that Tommy Moore's there. In the photo, one of the players I would have to look up is kneeling, palming the ball, his lips unnatural from the effort it's taking, his eyes proud all the same, and—I'm not just saying this—they do look like they could have won state. Austin should have driven that medal to us as well that year.

And, this time, unlike with the fire, it didn't matter where the deputies were from. Canadian Mounties could have looked through the wall of people not saying anything, seen Jonas King back there, the butt of a still-new .22 resting on the toe of his right shoe.

But no.

Where they finally found him was where he always went, where Belinda King had even let him pitch a tent a time or two on condition that he'd flash his lantern when she flashed the headlights.

It was back at the edge of the section their cul-de-sac had been cut into, right at the corner where the CRP met three fields of dryland. A little pad of concrete. The most important one in the world to him that year. Maybe ever.

And I say the Sherriff or his deputies found him out there, yeah. But it was his dad. Walking the whole way out, not even driving. Touching the heads of this piece of tall grass or that and leaving them be. Just making that connection over and over.

And the concrete pad, it was set in the middle of three of the older, deader trees in Midland County. Three trees that had been planted nobody was sure how long ago, as windbreak for the house that had stood there, had probably been there when the Reverends Green and Wood planted their cross a half mile to the west and a little south.

Way up high in the trees—you could see it now that they were pale, leafless enough for the sun to dry out—there was even iron of some kind, its rust bleeding down the bark. From a tree house? But tree houses seem so recreational, too. It's not what you think the covered wagon people had time for.

And the house, of course, it's long gone by 1985. Not even boards, just some of those nails with the angled-over heads, their shanks clotted with boles of rust. The occasional hinge, frozen closed. If you dig deep enough where the trash pile used to be, there's old-timey prescription bottles, more metal it would take a historian to identify.

I don't know.

I act like that's old, yeah, but I've talked to some of the old guys who have the stories from their childhoods, from the guys who were old to *them*. Stories about pushing cattle from Dallas to El Paso, how this country, from Midland up to Lubbock, there wasn't even a single house, fence, nothing. Maybe an Indian or two out there, the kind who couldn't believe in Oklahoma, but you don't ever see them if they don't want you to. All you ever do see, the whole day through, are east-facing dugouts in whatever slight rise there might be in the land. Dugouts people have evidently spent a winter in, the small, rounded openings black with soot, the punched-through chimneys long grown over.

As near as I can tell, though, none of those hands ever went into one of those dugouts and just sat there, pretended for a while. They had a job to do, I guess. A herd to tend. And now all those dugouts are caved in, plowed over.

And then there was the old timer I met in the back of a grocery store, who, sitting at a table half an hour later, bottles of coke between us—he must have bought them from the machine, because back then that's the only places bottles were anymore, and I never have change—he remembered going up to Palo Duro Canyon some Sundays growing up. How his grandpa then had been too old for horse work but wasn't dead yet, right? So they'd take the wagon down into the canyon floor, spend the day shoveling horse bones to haul to Amarillo, sell to the soap people. Indian horses. Another massacre.

And then my mom's dad, talking about when the Sandhill cranes changed their migration, started blotting the sky out over Stanton. How he went out and drew a bead on one with a .22, just to see how bad they tasted.

And then—then *his* dad, talking about when tractors first came to this part of the country. How all the old men, used to working behind a pair of mules, would still stand up at the end of each row, to pull back on the traces. How each time you could hear them cussing when they fell off the back of the tractor, and how, if you knew what was good for you, you never asked them about it later.

This is the great-grandfather who, when he cut most of his foot off working one day, made his way over to the neighbor's house and stood in her bathtub. He could have stood in his own, saved his own carpet, but then nobody would have ever found him.

Would he have known who used to live in that gone house they found Jonas at, though? Known whether the kids there went to Prairie Lee? How they got there? What Greenwood was like before the Reverends got there?

I doubt it.

And as for the concrete pad, it was a complete and wonderful mystery to Jonas. Rob King and Earl Holbrook's best guess, going by how it's shaped—more rectangular than square—and where it is, just off from where the house used to be, is that it's an old storm cellar. Except, of course, that the tops of those old cellars, they're not flat, are more bowed up, like they want to be domes. No clue why. Maybe a dome lasts longer than a flat roof, takes less crossbeams, or maybe it's so water won't stand there, leak down, or maybe it's just so you can stand up in the center of the room down there, I don't know.

The pad wasn't a dome by 1985, anyway. The concrete wasn't contemporary with the fallen-down house either, was smooth, had a "1971" dragged into it by a finger. Earl Holbrook, standing over it that first day with Rob and Jonas King—Holbrook was a cousin, married into the family, was always around for his year between farming and the gin—he looks away and says that more than likely, the house, after it got abandoned, the animals all started moving in. Which is no problem, usually. Unless a bobcat plops its bloody suitcase down one day, kicks everybody else out.

Even more than mountain lions, bobcats are something people in West Texas are always interested in. Mythical almost, all fifteen pounds of them. I only ever saw a couple—one darting out of my headlights, that I would have thought was a thick jackrabbit if my dad hadn't told me, and another on the bench seat of somebody's truck. The guy'd popped the mom with a shotgun, taken care of all the cubs. Except one. But still, he was having to wear welding gloves even for that cub, and it had already got through to his hand in a place or two.

His idea was to raise it, I think, like some people will when they shoot up a badger den or luck onto a baby raccoon while fishing—nobody's stupid enough to try to make a coyote into a dog, though I did have a friend with a pet javelina, and another with a possum in a hutch—but I didn't know the guy very well, didn't keep up. I'd guess it ran off the first chance it got, that cub, learning to live off the bobcat version of slow elk: cats and chickens. Which is when an old house can get to be a problem: when there's chicken feathers drifting across the wooden floor. A distinct feeling of contentment in the air.

Instead of going in with a shotgun or taking a match to the place, the thing to do, Earl Holbrook says, if you're thinking like an old man anyway, is to push the whole affair over into a ditch, bury it, the same as you do with old cars and twisted-up windmills. Or, if there's a collapsed cellar right there, then your job's already half-done, two birds with one scoop, all that. Just set your front-end loader up, pack the house down to ground level in that cellar, and then, to keep the cattle from breaking their legs for generations, cover the whole thing in whatever cement you've got handy. Maybe even smooth the top down, so whoever comes later will know this was intentional, not just a place some extra concrete got spilled back when.

It's what Jonas believed, anyway. A place almost as good as what the Phillips place will be for him someday.

Just a pad, though, that's nothing, no matter what you want to be buried under that pad.

No, what made the place *his* in the way it needed to be was that Earl Holbrook—Jonas' "uncle" since his other uncle was on all the roads but Cloverdale the last six months—had driven a six-inch pipe down at the eastern edge of the concrete, and clamped a backboard ten feet up it, helped Jonas measure out a free-throw stripe, spray paint a key, make hash marks about where the three-point line would be.

This is why the basketball goal up by the house was rusted, the net getting picked clean by birds.

Back here, Jonas could play whatever music he wanted. Flip the basket off when it spit his ball back. Cuss at it. Pee off the back corner, still standing on the concrete, the trucks passing on Cloverdale smaller than his pinky fingernail.

His brothers were still young enough that they couldn't come all the way back this far yet, too.

It was his.

Aside from Rob King standing back there, drinking a beer one day then hiding the bottle in the basketball pipe—Jonas has dropped rocks down there, heard more than one bottle break—and Earl Holbrook, to twist the backboard back straight after the big wind, and once, if he'd admit it, Belinda King, when Jonas fell asleep, forget to blink his lantern back, Jonas was the only one who'd been out there. In years, probably. The only one who knew that if he didn't keep that ball going, the snakes would come out of the grass in the afternoon to soak up the concrete's heat.

And then there were the old dead trees around it. Not a windbreak anymore, but still, thick enough that nobody could tell if he was there or not. And the sound of the ball didn't even carry across all that grass.

A perfect place if there ever was one. As close as you can find in West Texas, anyway.

Until Rob King walked up to it, the fingertips of his unbroken hand brushing the tops of the grass, so that Jonas wants to recite all the grass-judging he's been studying. Side-oats grama. Cane bluestem. Perennial threeawns.

All that's going away already, though.

This is just CRP grass. Filler, there to hold the dirt down.

Where we are now is the day after the shooting.

Jonas is dribbling, shooting, dribbling, dribbling, concentrating on making that next shot. That if he can swish it, then his dad walking up out of the field like he has been for the last two minutes, it'll just be a mirage.

But then he back-irons the shot.

Rob King takes a jog step forward, cuffs the ball up from the grass and nods once for Jonas to cut to the basket, son.

For a moment, just a moment, Jonas hesitates, and then he makes the cut, faking one way then taking the other, and his dad hits him with a crisp, one-handed pass and Jonas goes up textbook, and neither of them say anything, just run it over and over until finally the Sheriff has to come out for the both of them.

***

Five years later I'd get stopped in the rich residential over behind Midland Lee. Not pulled over but waved down at a roadblock we knew better than to back away from. Already that month we'd been chased down once, stopped in the Western Auto parking lot on the drag. Because we didn't have shirts maybe, the cops took apart the whole interior of the El Camino we were in, and dumped out all the cornflakes we'd been eating, just looking for a reason to haul us in.

There'd been nothing, though. Just a butterfly knife they flashed around, confiscated for their personal collection. Same old same old.

But that had been in the daylight, in a mostly legal car, with more cars always driving by. Now it was two in the morning, and we were in a blue Nova we'd just dropped a new engine into that afternoon, and there was nobody but us.

No knives this time, sure, but the two cruisers weren't parked across the road for random knife checks either. Somebody'd been breaking side glass all up and down the street, snatching stereo decks.

We all kind of sighed collectively—we were just passing through, going home, calling it a night—and the cops even shook their heads at the sloshy bottle of gin in the glove compartment that we hated but were drinking all the same. Then, just to be following procedure, they asked us to pop the trunk if we didn't mind, so we could be on our way.

We probably should have minded.

In there on a blanket were four stereos, wires going every which way from them.

It was a punch line. It made us a joke.

The police were not nice to us that night.

It's hardly the worst, though.

Another time, what was supposed to have been the last semester of my senior year at Greenwood, which had turned into a stint at Lee that went bad as well, they would stop me at the edge of town, for what I thought was just going to be the usual harassment—they knew my truck—but then the rest of the cops showed up as well. And then the detectives.

What they were interrogating me over was a Midland High cheerleader gone missing a few days back. Old news. What was new news was that they'd just found her in a cotton field on the north side of town. In pieces, in a hole.

And I was their guy, yeah. For hours and hours, until— and this is the only time this has ever happened, maybe in the whole history of these kinds of run-ins—my long hair saved me.

Trick was, the guy they had eyewitnesses for, the guy last seen with the cheerleader in a truck just like mine, he had shaved-short hair, high and tight. And while I could have had long hair when abducting this cheerleader, then taken the clippers to myself for a more straight-up look, I couldn't have gone the other way, from short to long.

So they took me back to my truck. Under the windshield were probably twenty notes, asking where I was, telling me where I should be. From everybody driving by. Some of them written on the back of beer bottle labels, or on the flaps of cases.

"Sorry," the detective said, not getting out of his car.

Yeah.

Later that year I'd be arrested on that same road, would find myself suddenly alone in booking for a moment, trying to pocket my mug shots, which would have been cool and great if the Sheriff—a different one than came for Jonas that day—hadn't noticed how blue my fingers were from whatever they used for mug shots.

Strike thirty-three, about.

It would be two years until my next arrest. Not two years for me to get hauled down to the station, locked in a room with a big mirror to study myself in, ashtrays to throw hard into the wall like I was the first one to ever think of that, but two years until the cuffs again, anyway. This time I wanted to fight, though. It was right outside Lubbock. I was going home to Midland for my brother's son, who had been dying since he was born, who, when he *was* born, I'd been on this same exact road, my four-hundred-dollar truck broke down from pushing it too hard, trying to make it to the hospital.

And if only I had.

But now this DPS, all he wanted was to drive me back to Lubbock, lock me in their tank, dare me to call Midland, pull somebody away from their grandchild, their nephew, just because I was in jail again.

Fuck him.

I'm glad all he had was a Camaro, so we had to sit right beside each other the whole ride back into town.

And even that wasn't the last time in. The last time, in a whole different part of Texas, I woke to a skinny guy on acid. He'd eaten it all to duck getting busted with it. TJ, initials for I don't know what. "Angel" in some other, better language. We were in the tank, some twelve of us, all strangers, none of our stories any different, really. I could have thrown a bottle at a cop car to get pulled in, I don't know. I remember thinking it that night, and having a bottle in my hand, so maybe. What TJ was doing when I woke was holding my head, his hand wrapped in as much of my hair as he could. He was trying to direct my vomit down into the drain. Only it wasn't vomit, but blood.

Afterward, I was shaking so hard that all twelve guys in the tank came over, gave me their blanket. My teeth still chattered, until I had to feel each one, see if it was broke. And then feel them all again.

Walking away the next morning, our court dates in our pockets, TJ bought me a honey bun with a dollar he somehow had (all my cash was in check form, from the city), laughed about the night before, and then there was a stroller suddenly by a dumpster. We took turns pushing it, ate the honey buns we hadn't thought to get napkins for, and I don't even know if I ever told him thanks. That this morning shouldn't have been happening at all.

As for where all of this started, though, I'm not stupid: 1985.

It changed all of us.

***

According to the Sheriff, it wasn't an interrogation in Rob King's living room that day. It wasn't an interrogation and it wasn't a boxing match, and it *damn* sure wasn't a tractor race. It was an interview. It was just to establish certain facts, not cast suspicion.

Still: "We're going to need that rifle, son."

This to Jonas King, whose voice wasn't something he could trust right then.

"He told you, Jim," Rob King said, "he lost it."

The Sheriff rolled his shoulders a bit, pulled his teeth from his lip as if this obvious lie was hurting him in some way, and said, "I'll be talking to the boy, Mr. King. If that's okay."

"You want Mr. King, his old ass is down the road there," Rob said back, at which point Belinda said his name, just once, *Rob*. And quiet. Not a warning, but so he could hear for himself what this was all building to. That the script of how this was all going to play out, it was right there in his tone already.

The Sheriff didn't say anything. Could probably see it all even better, right down to Rob falling across the driveway in cuffs, climbing up into his 4440, black smoke belching up into the chill, the front wheels popping up a foot or so when he dropped it into gear, the throttle already buried.

But that was all in a minute or two.

"So ask him," Rob King said, stepping aside, Jonas out in the open now.

"I lost it," Jonas said.

"See?" Rob King stepped back in front of the Sheriff.

Now the Sheriff smiled a bit, angled his mouth down to the CB on his shoulder. "Deputy Jenkins? Yeah, I'm going to need—"

"You can't pull me out of here," Rob King said, setting his feet, "the law, it says—"

"That one parent has to be present, Mr. King," the Sheriff completed, not bothering to look over when Deputy Jenkins stepped in through the front door, careful to wipe his boots on the mat, and make apology eyes to Belinda.

"Rob, if you'll just—" he said.

Rob King laughed. "You're escorting me out of my own damn house, here? Am I missing something?"

"*Rob*," Belinda said again.

It wasn't enough.

Before that day, the worst violence that had ever happened in the Kings' living room, it had involved battery cases that wouldn't come off new toys, precision screwdrivers that poked forward into the meat of somebody's hand.

Now, though. Now Belinda was going to need some new carpet.

As for Jenkins, that's not his real name. Because I promised way earlier not to use their real names.

But it's close enough.

When he touched Rob King's sleeve to guide him out, Rob King laid him out. And I know "righteous" is the wrong word here, is too celebratory, doesn't show the proper respect to the law, but—Jonas remembers his dad coming home once from a sale, the pinky and ring finger of his right hand broke. Because somebody in a convenience store had said something to him about his wife, Jonas' mom, and Jonas' dad's hand (the way Rob King told it) had come sailing through the air before he could even tell it to make itself all the way into a fist.

At the store that day, though, Rob King just paid for his coke, walked out.

There weren't any other deputies to call in, I mean. There weren't nightsticks in the general vicinity.

After it was done and Rob's already broke hand wouldn't stop bleeding, the Sheriff shook his head in disappointment, called in an ambulance just to cover his ass.

"Sorry you had to see that, ma'am," the Sheriff said to Belinda King, who was holding Jonas to her side, and to Jonas, just staring at his dad in cuffs on the living room carpet, his eyes wild, air coming in rasps, shirt untucked in exactly the way Rob King was always warning Jonas about. "We might should just station the paramedics down at the church, think?" the Sheriff went on. "Just for him, and everything he thinks he can do."

Insert a picture of Belinda King here, just staring at him.

The Sheriff smiled his good-old-boy smile, pinched his uniform pants up his thighs enough to lean down a smidge, say to Jonas, "Now, son, I just—"

"He told you," Belinda said, pushing Jonas behind her. "He lost that rifle."

At which point the Sheriff peeled his wide hat off, ran his hand through what was left of his hair.

"Let's," he said, and opened the door for Deputy Gaylord, ushered Rob King out, guiding his head through the door, being sure to tell Gaylord to keep an eye on this one, that he might go rabbit.

Gaylord laughed like "fat chance" and the Sheriff twisted the dead bolt shut.

"I lost it," Jonas King said, right when that bolt drove home.

"Son," the Sheriff said, disappointed.

"It's time for you to leave my house," Belinda King said then.

"Ma'am, Lindy—"

"*Please.*"

"I just, I just need to," he said, reaching around her a bit, to pull Jonas back into view.

He didn't plan on Belinda's knee, though.

Or that she would follow him down, tooth and claw.

"*Run!*" she said back to Jonas, frozen there on the bloody carpet, "go, go, go," and Jonas did, Jonas does, two miles through the field to his grandfather's, to hide in the tack shed that's already fallen down, already smells like porcupine. It's not the deputies that find him that night either, but Arthur King's five dogs.

Two days later Arthur King will unceremoniously shoot all five of them, even the one that takes off across the field. The reason he gives is that they got into a skunk. Their names: Blackie and Cotton and Slim and Prince and Ranger. Prince is the last of a series of litters going back nearly forty-five years, to Mouse's time. He almost makes it across the field, too.

There are no graves for them, just this.

***

In the best of the series of photographs from the day of the shooting, 1985, you can see the team bus, two DPS cars, the Sheriff's cruiser, and farmers' trucks lined almost all the way back to the church, out of the frame.

The basketball players are all already gone, of course, Geoff Koenig sirened away by ambulance—yeah, if there'd been one by the church, it wouldn't have hurt—Coach Harrison taking that ride with him. Leonard just walking back to the school, across the field. The bus is a crime scene now, won't be moved for days. The keys are still in it.

Of the farmers milling around in the ditch, waiting to volunteer whatever they can, there's no Rooster, no Arthur King, no Rob King. And the ones who are there, they all look so young. Like, in the two or three years between that day and when I would be old enough to start working for them, they would have aged fifteen years.

Or maybe it was just around me that they seemed older. Like they were letting me run a few hours on their 4440s out of duty, more or less, a burden of obligation that weighed on them, aged them around the eyes because when they looked at me they saw me standing there and they saw me as I had been, too.

The money was the same, though. For a while.

In that photograph—in all of them—most of the farmers are either looking into the ditch or out across the fields. Waiting for that next shot, maybe. Macy Barnes is there, his shirt white and ironed, a businessman at the beginning of the day and a businessman at the end. I always half-expected him to have a briefcase. There's Gary Wilkes squinting against the sun, a stem of grass fixed between his teeth like he's posing for a postcard. Michael Graham's dad, Rex Allen—no clue why you always had to say his middle name, just that you did—his signature Dr. Pepper in his right hand, his dentures loose in his mouth.

Used to, whenever his wife would look away he'd wow his eyes out, thrust his teeth out on his purple stub of a tongue. Earl Holbrook, in the brown collar-shirt everybody was wearing that year at the gin, so you could tell who was working there, who was just hanging around for peanuts and coffee. Clete Jennings, staring out across the field to the south, where most of his fields still were. Maybe staring to see if there was going to be smoke this day or not. Martin Ledbetter, in long pants for once, his eyes hidden behind sunglasses that probably cost eighty dollars, had a matching alligator case on the dash of his truck. Pete Manson, a cigarette always to his lips, his wedding ring on the middle finger of his left hand, because his ring finger's a nub.

Of all of them, he's the only one who never looks across all the stalks, for that next shot.

Chapter Seven

The one person Rob King would never talk about was Sterling. His suicide brother.
I think I understand.
My nephew who was dying a few pages ago, that was the first time I've said anything about him in all these years.
His name was ~~Dallas~~. His name was ~~Houston~~.
It was Austin.
He was the first grandkid, the golden child, the same as Sterling had been, and Mouse before him.
Ms. Godfrey would have an explanation for that, I guess. A footnote or a play or a literary tradition.
She doesn't know everything, though.
She doesn't know that I used to save my fingernails, say. In a Tylenol bottle, back when everyone was sure every third Tylenol pill was poison. By fifteen, that little white bottle was almost full. Until my littlest brother found it when I was gone one day. I scooped what I could back into the bottle, stormed down the hall to my room, slammed the door hard enough that it would sound locked, anyway.
Two hours later, cooled down, I would open that door again. There on the carpet was my littlest brother's apology: he'd found

some clippers, cut all his own nails off. Deep, so that each one was bloody. Him waiting down the hall to see for himself that everything was okay now. It wasn't.

Another thing Ms. Godfrey doesn't know is that, moving up to Colorado, I finally had to let go of the backboard I'd been carrying with me from house to house ever since I left Greenwood. It was all warped and scarred, just the ghost of a red square on it anymore, and it took all kinds of mismatched washers and carriage bolts to even keep a rim up there, but still, each time I was fading away from it, in whatever driveway was mine at the time, I felt like I was still me. Like if I just made this shot, then everything would be all right, that I could keep the world together by placing that ball through the net one more time.

And she especially doesn't know about Buddy.

My dog about four years ago, a golden boxer some eight-months old, with parvo.

We fed him goat milk and Enfamil and Gatorade and everything we could think of, but still, he was going, until one night it was time to shoot him. Except, up in the top of my closet, I didn't have any more shells. Not in the ashtray of my truck either, and not in the pockets of any of my jackets, and not behind the *seat* of my truck, and not the ashtray again either, though I checked and checked, insisted. It was two in the morning already, the stores were closed, everybody I knew sleeping.

But still.

You can do it with a narrow rope if you have to, a parachute cord you bought at Army surplus because it only cost a dollar. You can do it if you don't mind having that feel of muscle dying under your hands, the way it creaks like it's drying out. You can do it if you don't mind having that feeling in your hands for the rest of your life.

To even get there, though, what you have to do is dig deeper into your closet, for the mule-eared boots you haven't tried to fit into for years.

They make it feel more like a movie, what you're doing. Like you're walking into a scene here. Like your lines are already all laid out for you, your actions blocked out. Like there's some director watching you, nodding yes, that this is right, this is good, everybody quiet now.

Never mind the actor there, his knee between the dog's shoulder blades.

I'm not going into that backyard again, though.

But it's not always just a backyard, either. Sometimes it's a whole county.

My favorite dog when I was twelve, one Friday afternoon when we were going to the lake, I couldn't find her and couldn't find her. Finally, when none of his excuses were getting us out of the house, my dad told my mom the story. They were in the garage, which is like trying to whisper in a cave. This is what he didn't know I was hearing: that his buddy from way back, our neighbor, had gotten understandably tired of Sheba chasing his van every day, so had finally stopped that morning, turned that Chevy van around and chased the dog instead. All through the pasture, wider and wider loops, until he caught her. The fresh ruts were right there, obvious, would be for years. After he hit Sheba, then, she got up and kept running, made one more giant loop, going for all she was worth, then came back to the van, fell over in some kind of shock, her side rising shallow and fast. This was good, I thought, about to round the corner. She'd lived. It was what she always did. Except. Instead of scooping her into the back of the truck, my dad and the neighbor—Gene, Gene, *Gene*, I can't say it enough times—put her in a plastic trash bag, dug a hole for her so that she probably didn't die until she woke up.

We didn't make the lake that weekend. They didn't find me that night until almost dawn, and that was just because I didn't have a driver's license yet, or a flip switch to blow the world up.

Then my next dog, Pepper, a lanky tall black and brown goof who'd wandered up especially to help me be thirteen. At a barbecue one Sunday, one of my young cousins was petting one of the other dogs, and Pepper growled like he always did. Not at my little cousin—taller than me now—but at the other dog, for getting attention. It didn't matter. My cousin's dad heard, cocked his head to be sure he'd heard, then took two steps over to his car, leaned in through the open window, his cheeseburger plate balanced in his other hand the whole time. When he turned back around, he was leading with his nickel-plated .38. There in the middle of all of us, so we felt the spray even if it didn't stain our clothes, he took half of Pepper's head off, from the left eye back, and said it in the silence that followed, before we all started breathing again: that *no* dog was going to growl at his kid, by God. By the time the men came back from burying Pepper, the cheese on our burgers was cold, and none of the women were talking to any of the men, and I didn't even run away, just sat there under the clothesline, staring out across the pasture.

All of which is to say that that night with Buddy, I should have known, should have been more ready. And it's not like I hadn't been shooting deer and elk and everything else in all the years before Buddy—a horse once, even, that I had to run away from, am still running away from—and not like I hadn't sawed the heads off just-dead Hereford bulls, for their skulls, and dug through rotting cows for their elbow calluses and eye lenses, which I was collecting for a while, and not like

I hadn't killed who knows how many birds and snakes and rabbits by then, but Buddy—his name was no accident. That's the best way to say it, maybe. He was Sheba and Pepper and the rest, only safe, far from Greenwood.

I don't know.

I sat on the back porch with him for two days while he was dying, didn't even read, and when he started peeing just sitting there, so that it ran onto both of us, his ears back from embarrassment, the pee still Enfamil practically, I told him it was all right, that it was all going to be all right, and just sat there with him some more, making promises, offering trades.

You don't get to save them all though, I don't guess. Even the important ones.

You'd think I'd have learned that by then.

***

From their back window—this is still two weeks before Stacy Monahans' funeral, which would change everything—Belinda King and her sons watch the Sheriff's men move through the CRP all around their cul-de-sac.

What the windbreakered men are after is the .22.

Not that there's a slug to match it to yet, or any witnesses, but still, if that little Savage .22 fell out of the horse scabbard bolted to the pushbar and fender of the three-wheeler like Jonas says, then the Sheriff's department wants to see it lying there in the grass. Know that it hasn't been hidden.

It'll mean everything.

If they don't find it, too.

"Mom," Jonas says.

Belinda King just stands there. Not tuned out, but tuned all the way in, it seems. Completely.

The Sheriff's men are sifting through the blown-up pump house now.

"Wait here," she says to him finally, "watch your brothers," and then's stalking out there, is going to tell Deputy Jenkins something, except before she can get there Rob King is rounding the corner.

The Sheriff's with him.

Rob's whole arm is in a sling now.

They're two days out from the first interview. The first time Rob's been back since then.

There'll be no charges, so long as he cooperates from here on out. His second free pass in as many months, like he's charmed.

Ask him, you might get a different answer.

But there are moments like these, too.

Belinda goes to him and he hugs her with the arm he has, looks over her shoulder to the sliding back door. His sons are there, each in pants, hair combed to the side.

He'd called ahead, from the station, his voice the kind of muffled and insincere that meant he wasn't alone.

Fluttering in his hand is the warrant signed by one of Martin Ledbetter's golf buddies. It's for the whole section of CRP, neighbors' yards included, but it's for the house too.

Everybody's so apologetic.

Rob even crosses the backyard, shakes Deputy Jenkins' left hand, taking him away from the pump house long enough for them to talk about it like it's getting rebuilt anytime soon. Like Jonas won't be out there come October, wrapping the pipes against the cold.

Behind them, the trampoline is becoming part of the old fence.

Farther out than that, across the field, leaning against a white post on his porch, Arthur King is drawing a cigarette to his lips, the first in fifteen years. Though it's not what he intends for it to do, the smoke will clear his wife's eyes for the morning and she'll be her old self, except she'll think it's 1968.

He won't correct her.

***

As for how Rooster knew about Junior and Mouse, knew about Walter Jr.'s predilections, I never questioned it. But, from what I've heard about Mouse, it wouldn't be like him to say anything bad about the family. The Kings have always been close-to-the-vest like that. At eighteen, the information itself was jarring enough that I didn't even think to question it. Only kind of wished I didn't have to know.

Now, though, to keep from suspecting that he made it up, that him and Arthur King were that deep of enemies, what I have to imagine is that Rooster and Mouse weren't just in the same squadron or troop or whatever the Army has. What I have to imagine is that maybe Rooster knew Mouse when he was young, somehow, even though Rooster only seems to have moved into Greenwood later in life, with money he got from the lawsuit after his work truck fireballed up all around him.

Maybe he'd been here before, though.

Maybe he grew up around Greenwood, made the kind of exit nobody noticed or would have cared about if they had, then, his ear melted off but his bank account full of blood money, he came back, started buying up the community that had ignored him growing up.

Real Victor Hugo, yeah. But it's got to be something like that.

If he had known Mouse as a kid, anyway, then it would have been easier to see, I think. Just in Mouse's behavior. Not that there are specific tells for that kind of stuff, I don't think, at least to the untrained, but—if Rooster's home life wasn't quite ideal either, if he'd heard those same boots in the hall before, then maybe he could pick something up from Mouse. The way he acted, the front he put up. The smile he was known for.

Somehow, Rooster knew the truth about the Kings.

And Mouse, I think—you always want a witness, somebody who understands, who can nod that this is good, yes, this makes sense—he *knew* Rooster knew. It was why he was finally able to stand up in that field of grass in Germany or Italy or France or whatever made-up place it was.

For him, I know, it was the yellow grass of an empty field in Greenwood, spreading out all around him, all the way back to Prairie Lee.

He was home. His friend from second grade was here, the tremble in the ground wasn't tanks but tractors, and he was home.

When Rooster told me the story of it that one time, his old man lips were curled into a smile, but they were tight, too. Unsure. Like he was trying to give shape to something that at the time, for him, had had no shape, was too big for words.

If he'd heard those boots in the hall, I mean, then what's to keep him from standing up along with Mouse that day?

This is key, I think.

What can keep you from doing what Mouse did, it's not strength or will or duty to those you'd leave behind, any of that, it's that the family you come from, nobody would be surprised what was going on behind those closed doors. Maybe everybody even just assumes it, and lets it go.

It makes your world make sense, kind of.

Makes you want to come back, show them all.

If you're Mouse, though, and your dad, he's a deacon, a booster, a landowner, legitimate West Texas gentry, then what you never can wrap your head around, it's this division between the daytime world and the nighttime one. Not how blind everybody can be, but how these two worlds you're living in, they don't fit together, *can't* fit together.

So one day you finally see a crack between them, and stand up into it, and this is it, the calm place you knew had to exist.

Of course you smile, standing there. A little bit with wonder. This is it, what you've been waiting for.

Mouse.

I never knew him, but still.

Some people you don't have to.

***

That day of the search, what the six men from the Sheriff's department finally found wasn't the .22, but it didn't help, either.

Back in Jonas' bedroom, high in his closet where his brothers couldn't reach, was an olive-green index-card box. Keeping it closed were two red rubber bands, longways—not flat rubber bands that like to break, but the squarish ones that last—then one dried-out tan one around the middle. They were security, were wrapped that way—red-then-tan-then-red again, on top—so that Jonas would know if anybody'd been in there.

Until the day of the search, no one had.

The tan rubber band did its job, broke. But then the deputy just walked in, gave the box to the Sheriff. Didn't care about getting caught. Had a warrant, I guess, could break whatever rubber bands he wanted to.

At the kitchen table, Jonas sat up a little straighter.

Belinda was across from him, her youngest in her lap.

"What?" she said.

Jonas shook his head no, nothing.

At the kitchen table now, the Sheriff sighed. Studied a candle mounted on the wall, maybe. Something over there. But there was no answer, no good way to do this.

What he pulled up from the box once it was quiet enough was four arrowheads, three of them found in a sandstorm off 137 just south of Lamesa with Earl Holbrook. Jonas and Earl had had to wear swim goggles the whole afternoon, walking up and down the rows that were blowing away. The fourth was bought for fifty cents at a flea market, was perfectly shaped, could never kill anything.

Next were the front-elbow calluses from a series of dead cows, and after that was an unspent token from the Gold Mine Arcade, with a pinhole drilled through it, one just wide enough to pass twelve-pound test through.

Jonas winced but the Sheriff just set it aside, reached deeper into the box.

What he came up with this time, what the deputy had probably already told him was there, was one photograph and two medals. The photograph was old and brown and curling at the edges, was of a smiling, lanky seventeen-year-old kid from two generations ago, standing at an impossible angle by a tack shed fallen all the way over now. And the medals—Jonas had to look away.

The medals had turned up missing from Jonas' grandmother's sewing kit two Thanksgivings ago. And, between the turkey and football and dishes, she'd noticed. Meaning she was always slipping off to hold them, be sure they were there? What other explanation could there be.

She'd called the Sheriff in (that was how he knew what they were), but before he got there, everybody had had told her that those weren't Sterling's medals, Sterling had never gone to war.

That she must be confused. That she was the right age to be confused.

But she insisted he had. That he was a hero, had been fighting for them all.

It wasn't a good Thanksgiving.

Jonas threw up from nerves back by the shop, and the dogs, Prince and Blackie and the rest, darted in to lick it up.

It's what he feels like doing now, too, not just from the sad way his mom's looking at him, but from the way the Sheriff's holding those two medals up like spectacles, to look through, his eyes black and glinty behind the neat bullet hole in each. The bullet holes that can, presumably, be matched to other bullet holes.

Four years later, if the Sheriff's horse suddenly dies, Jonas isn't going to know anything about it. And none of his friends will either. And they'll never go back to that pasture again.

Chapter Eight

The goats. I was lying earlier, I think, about that tractor and sunflower story being the first story I ever got noticed for.

The year before, I won an award for a personal essay I'd done for some composition course. It was supposed to have been just filler, done at the last possible hour—the T.A. was soft—but when you don't have enough time, it's hard to make things up enough. To disguise them like you need to.

The essay was about goats, but it was more, too.

Me and my dad were supposed to be watching the neighbor's goats while he took his family to Six Flags. It was just goats, though; my dad gave me twenty dollars in advance for the four-day weekend, and borrowed a three-wheeler for me, my first, so I could ride over in the mornings, keep the goats in water and feed, wrestle with the boss goat now that Mr. Mercer wasn't around to disapprove.

It wasn't my fault either, what happened.

Dogs.

Later, in high school, one of my friends would weld a shop-made cowcatcher of pipe two feet in front of his bumper, just for plowing through the packs of dogs that kept happening. Chase them through the fields when they got too smart to come up onto the road. Why they were happening was that, during the boom, everybody in Midland had bought these big horse-dogs, showpieces really, but then got tired of the feeding, the mess, and what else do you do with a dog you don't want, right? They brought them to us. The country. Greenwood.

The result was all these motley packs of Labradors and Rottweilers, Irish Setters and every kind of Shepherd. Probably good-natured at one time, but hungry now, and thinking like a pack, not like pets. I didn't have that big bumper on my truck, though, and was broke down so much it wouldn't have mattered if I did. One Friday, even, the first semester of my senior year, I'm walking in a ditch well after midnight, my truck ticking down a mile or two behind me, a new dent kicked in its flank, when I hear them moving through the mesquite alongside me. The dogs. I broke immediately, slinging off my hat, my belt, anything to get them to stop even for a moment, and ran faster than I've ever run, until I was able to plant a boot on the brick planter in front of this house out in the middle of nothing, vault my midsection up into the eave, pull myself the rest of the way up. Stay there beating on the roof and throwing shingles at the dogs until my mom came slow down the road a few hours later, looking for me dead, like I think she always expected.

That goes both ways, though.

The year before the fire, when she'd go shopping at Albertson's on Wednesday nights, I'd work myself into a panic each time, finally sneaking in to call the store, have her paged, then, when that didn't work, gathering my little brother—usually having to drag him out of bed—and sitting by the window that faced Midland, making us hold hands so that when we prayed for her to make it back, it would be magnified by two, anyway.

I was twelve, yeah. Maybe even eleven.

Sometimes my dad would catch us like that and just lean against the door jamb, shake his head.

It worked, though, right?

But the dogs. They'd scattered the neighbor's goats through the fence. Two of them they'd pulled down, one by the neck, dead already, and one hamstrung. Neither really eaten on that much, because they were domestic dogs, had the wrong instincts for all of this, but not exactly in the shape Mr. Mercer wanted them kept in either.

I buzzed the three-wheeler back to my mom, told her, and she went to the porch, studied the horizon to the north, then did that kind of mental calculus all farmers' wives learn, the kind that plots out what field their husband *said* they were going to be in, but allowing for about six hundred variables, any one of which can lead to another and another, eventually land them in a strange tractor in some other field altogether.

The dust she was seeing about a mile off, I mean, it wasn't necessarily going to be my dad.

But it was there or nowhere, too.

"Okay," she said, my little brothers at Vacation Bible School that week (this was my first year off—thank you, Mr. Mercer), and, instead of driving the long way around to flag him down, she stepped out of her shoes, told me to get back to the goats, keep them out of the road as best I could.

"But—" I started.

But I wasn't supposed to go in the ditch.

She didn't hear, was already walking away the way she still did sometimes back then, barefoot, taking the caliche road to Cloverdale at first, chancing the ditch, then stepping into that good soft dirt of a plowed field. It was the only way to do it, she'd tell us. Otherwise your shoes fill up with dirt, right? And anyway, she'd grown up barefoot in cotton fields, her mom sending her out to fetch her dad for dinner most nights.

My dad had warned her about walking around like that—snakes, chemicals, goat heads, white weeds, stalks left over from last season, fiberglass storage tanks spread out by the wind—but she didn't care, and I think he liked finding her in the turnrow sometimes.

I buzzed back to the Mercers', tried to get the hamstrung goat to drink some water, like that could help, and then we both looked up. There was a chainsaw in the air. My dad, on some impossible Yamaha three-wheeler he'd commandeered. I laid the goat's head back down, rode out to meet him, and we spent the rest of the time before lunch screaming and laughing and coughing in the ditch, chasing one goat back through the hole just to have another skate out onto the asphalt. Dust and grass so thick in the air that we could hardly see each other sometimes. The way I wrote it in that essay—I don't have it anymore—the way I wrote the end of it is that everything then, the dirt in the sunlight, it was golden, it was perfect, and then I closed that shutter, just let that day stay like that.

That night, my dinner wrapped in foil on the seat of the three-wheeler I was already in love with, the hamstrung goat would finally die, its head on my lap. The dogs barking out in the draw, waiting.

With the rifle I was about go home and ask for as matter-of-factly as I could, I lined up on each one of them, pulled the trigger until I was out of make-believe shells, so that when they came for me six or seven years later, I knew to run, and not to stop.

***

The next game for the basketball team is eleven days into 1986. A tournament Greenwood's hosting. All the other teams' buses parked in the high school parking lot at exactly the same angle: Colorado City, Iraan, Big Lake, Stanton, Monahans, maybe one more.

Greenwood's not just short Tommy Moore now, our star, but Geoff Koenig, who'd averaged eight points per game the year before. All of them trash, sure, no plays ever run directly for him, but still. Instead of all seniors, there's a junior and a sophomore in the starting lineup, even after Coach gave his big lecture about no more lower classmen moving up, even if we made regionals.

Before Greenwood's first game there's a moment of silence for Tommy and Geoff. Some of the high schoolers hold their lighters up like a concert but get their arms guided back down. Fire's where it all started, after all. They're not doing it in bad taste, but, most of them not being eighteen yet, there's no good reason for them to *have* those lighters either, right?

They have good intentions anyway.

Tommy Moore's mom cries in thanks, and everybody pretends not to see her. If you do, then you might have to say something. Mr. Moore isn't there to put his arm around her, either, and Ms. Godfrey's probably standing in their driveway at that exact moment, making promises to herself. That she'll never leave Tommy after this, never, no matter what.

The only Kings at the tournament are Earl Holbrook and his wife Sissy, though nobody really considers them Kings, even though Earl did lose two modules in the fire. *Arthur King lost an even twenty.* Earl had already been at the gin that morning, though, had been for most of the night, only got back to his modules after the volunteer fire department had blown them apart with water, then raked them into the dirt looking for coals.

Where Earl and Sissy sit every game is half court, six rows up, right where the seats change color, so they're each in a different one, reaching across the middle for popcorn, coke. To hold hands.

The only King-by-*name* in attendance at the tournament is Jonas, his three-wheeler hidden back by the field house, the spark plug in his pocket like his dad taught him.

So everybody will know he's ridden in, not just been dropped off by his mom, he's keeping his Honda-red helmet cocked under his arm, has his jeans tucked into the heavy motorcycle boots he's going to have to grow into. They make his steps large and deliberate, make him want to see the shadow he's throwing here, how epic it has to be.

In the concession-stand crush before tip-off—no accident he waited until then—he places the helmet up on the counter to pay for his frito pie so that the booster handing him his seventy-five cent coke has to call him back to get it, his helmet.

It's only then he realizes that that's the first anybody's spoken to him. Even his friends. They haven't said anything about his boots, his dad, any of it. He's not even sure they're there.

What he does instead of cruising the visitor stands with them like usual is sit in the cafeteria and spork his food in, make his coke last until the second quarter and flinch more than he means to when the ball slaps the glass by his table. Then he notices that everybody on the Greenwood side is watching. Not the game, not the ball being thrown back in fifteen feet away, but *him,* Jonas King.

The spark plug is hot in his front pocket.

He lowers his face to his coke, tells himself he's just making things up, and pulls the last drink halfway up the straw and holds it there. The trade is that if he can do it like that for a ten-count, a twenty even, the coke just standing there against all common sense, then when he finally lets it go, everything will be all right again.

Sixteen counts later, Earl Holbrook sits down across from him.

Jonas lets the coke back down the straw.

Earl still has his gin-shirt on, has come straight from work, met Sissy there like every game night. They don't have any kids in 1986, and won't later either. Jonas' mom knows Earl Holbrook from Lamesa, though he'd been a few years ahead of her, and she remembers Sissy as well, from her own grade, but mostly because of her big brother, always beating everybody up. Stories Belinda just shakes her head about.

Rob isn't so shy, though. The story he told Jonas about Larry—Sissy Monahans' big brother—was that once he had come to the drive-in with a four-way lug wrench, of all things, taken on four Mexicans at once, their lowrider included, and that was when he was just a sophomore, still had two more years of legends to cut.

In the pictures I've seen of Stacy Monahans (in the paper, at her funeral, in the Tornado yearbook), she doesn't have Larry's lantern jaw at all, but takes after her mother, Gwen: blonde hair, easy smile, eyes like a deer. None of the nervousness Gwen always had about her, that Jonas' mom would never talk about either.

That said enough, though. That Gwen *hadn't* always been nervous like that. That she had once been like her daughter, dating a boy too tall, unsure where to put his hands, his eyes always looking somewhere else, like you might know what he's thinking otherwise.

She's still around, too. I could ask her, I guess. But I won't. I can't.

As for how her daughter Stacy Monahans, the untouchable girl from Lamesa, ever met Geoff Koenig, the soon-to-get-shot basketball star in Greenwood, it was the usual: Arthur King was paying Geoff by the hour to scythe down the weeds on his property that couldn't be got to with a shredder, then to hoe up the ones a scythe couldn't reach, and Stacy had been down with her dad's single-horse trailer, running barrels in Arthur King's new blue arena.

Drop a girl as blonde as her in the same section as any sixteen-year-old boy, I mean, and he'll find her inside of ten minutes, then just stand at the fence, his gloved hands cocked over the pipe, every last bit of his attention on the way her knees clamp onto that sorrel horse, her hat pulled down low like all the barrel girls do.

And Geoff, he was like all the boys in Lamesa, had to have been—rangy, dark, shaggy in the summer, quick to smile, slow to talk—but he wasn't *from* there, either, hadn't known Stacy in second grade, when she used to always wear those lime-green tights every day she could sneak them out of the house.

It matters.

For Rob and Belinda, it had gone the same way, the girl in Lamesa, the boy from Greenwood, the two of them meeting at the Dairy Treat in Stanton when they could, at the rocket park after dark when they couldn't. It had been the same for Earl and Sissy Holbrook, even, though Earl had been a Lamesa Golden Tornado until his junior year, his parents divorcing. They'd all met in the same choreographed ways too, like there was some agreement between the communities, to keep trading bodies back and forth, keep the blood fresh.

Jonas the product of some of that trading.

He can't imagine ever living in Lamesa, though. It's a whole different world. The moon, practically.

Case in point: Six years later, his truck will break down there and he'll walk into town. Like they've been waiting for him all month, then, five cops will swoop in, voices raised, guns out, thinking he either just robbed the convenience store or is just *about* to. Same old same old. They don't believe him until he takes them back to his truck, either, and for once he remembers to not let them search it. It's because of the pistol under the bench seat, that he almost went back for, in case Lamesa had dogs too.

Sometimes the gods smile, I mean.

The tournament, though.

What Jonas is doing now, since Earl Holbrook sat down across from him, is watching his frito pie bag uncrinkle, the leftover chili slowing it down some. It's a tin flower, blooming.

Watching it, Jonas wonders what he would look like if he were someone else, a kid with blond hair, a gold rope chain around his neck.

It would be perfect.

He wouldn't care about frito pie bags at all, then. Wouldn't have to.

"Fourteen points," Earl Holbrook says, placing his open hand on the table. Saying something because Jonas isn't.

Fourteen is how far Greenwood's already behind. *Six*teen now.

Like any team can climb back from that in the third quarter, never mind one with just three bodies on the bench.

"Single elimination?" Jonas says, though he knows.

Earl nods, Jonas nods. All of Greenwood nodding.

"Backboard's doing that thing again," Jonas throws out, tilting his flat hand back and forth. He's talking about the backboard leaning over his concrete pad. "Maybe Robert'll let me back the truck up, you know?"

It's what he calls his dad around Earl. Mostly because it's what Earl calls Rob King. A joke of some kind, one Jonas has never quite got a handle on.

Standing on the toolbox of his truck is how Earl tightens the u-bolts on Jonas' backboard, anyway. Meaning Jonas will need a truck if he wants to tighten them himself.

"Maybe we'll put lock washers on *both* sides this time," Earl says, his eyes on the game, then pulls his hand into a fist when one of the three T's dribbles off his foot.

Time-out.

A minute fifty-four left until halftime.

Where Earl and Sissy live is in a trailer way back behind the water station. The two-deep line of trailers where that roughneck who's supposed to have a black panther in his freezer lives, where the pasture's never been plowed into CRP, so that, his junior year, Jonas and his best friend can go out there with white gas, pump it into the holes, sell the rattlesnakes that come up at two and a half dollars per pound.

Way out in that pasture too, once, there'll be a dull silver tanning bed, almost new. For no reason at all, its cord tucked up into the bed part. Like somebody just didn't want the bank to get it, maybe. It'll look Egyptian, for some pharaoh way in the future. Even though it'll be the summer they're shooting everything, hawks and porcupines and transformers, anything stupid enough to get in range, still, they won't shoot that tanning bed.

"You see how that LaFayette kid always cuts on the weak side?" Earl says to Jonas.

Again: he doesn't have any kids of his own.

Jonas shrugs, looks around.

Pete Manson's the first person he sees. Just standing there at the glass with his paper boat of nachos, the jalapeños self-serve, mounded on. Jonas has to look away from Pete's finger stub, can't imagine how he'd ever eat anything if his hand looked like that.

Pete Manson nods, smiles around his nachos at Jonas.

"What?" Earl says, half-turning in his Ranger-blue chair.

"He only cuts when they're in high-post," Jonas says, bringing Earl back.

Earl smiles, narrows his eyes, then shakes his head in wonder the next time LaFayette makes his cut.

"You're going to show them all, aren't you?" he says, taking Jonas' helmet up, studying the empty face.

It's what everybody's been saying to Jonas already, since he started getting his height, his legs.

Jonas smiles, says inside, *yes*.

When you're thirteen, it's always *yes*.

"Need anything?" Earl asks then, standing, his elbow cocked back, hand to his wallet.

Jonas shakes his head no, scrapes the helmet back across the table, turns the empty face around, very aware that Earl isn't leaving. Is just standing there.

Finally he says it down to Jonas, what he's been working up to: "It's all going to be all right, you know?"

It makes Jonas' eyes hot.

Because he's afraid his voice might crack, he thins his lips and nods that he knows. That of course it'll be okay. Then he swallows. It feels loud enough that everybody has to hear it.

When he comes back to Earl, Earl's seen all this.

"Cool?" he says to Jonas.

"Cool," Jonas manages to get out, and then Earl nods again, salutes Jonas as he's walking away, the horn in the gym blowing, the crowd swelling with noise.

Jonas goes to his straw for another drink of nothing, and Pete Manson's still watching him. Pete raises his red cup to toast Jonas, sort of. To wish him well.

Jonas nods back as little as possible.

In 1986 Pete Manson doesn't have any kids either, and won't.

Jonas sits through the next dilated minute and a half of play—*three* twenty-second timeouts, the coaches reckless for some reason—doesn't look back to Pete Manson but keeps looking the other way, like he's expecting somebody. His uncle, in off the road. His grandfather, coming to his first district game in years. Tommy Moore on crutches, walking like the most careful spider.

Instead it's just somebody with a briefcase phone, trying to balance it on his shoulder while he pays his two dollars for a ticket.

It looks fake, the phone, like a military radio in a World War II movie, and Jonas tracks the guy across the cafeteria, the guy walking with his head up, looking for somebody. Like anything's important enough to interrupt the first varsity game of the new year.

Jonas balls his frito bag up again, flinches when the buzzer crashes down all around him, Leonard holding the button down painfully long, and then the stands are emptying into the cafeteria for halftime. Jonas just sits at his table at first but nobody's talking to him again, so he takes his helmet, deposits his trash in the farthest-away can, hoping to run into somebody, then weaves his way back past the concession stand, aiming for the bathrooms, where he won't look so alone—where you're supposed to be alone, just standing there, looking at nothing. But they're too full, already have a line snaking down the hall.

Just thirty feet down from them, though, where the hall goes carpet, becomes lockers and classrooms, the aluminum gate that's usually pulled down, it's only pulled down most of the way. Not enough to lock.

Jonas takes his lower lip into his mouth, knows where another bathroom is, yes.

To get there, he has to dawdle at the water fountain until nobody's really looking, then retie his (buckle-only) boots back in the shadows, then step deeper, go belly-down on his fingertips, slide under the gate.

When he reaches back to pull his helmet after him, though, it's too tall. By an inch, maybe less.

"Shit," he hisses, his new word, and is about to lay it over on its side to angle it under, make his big escape, when suddenly there's a low-cut white sneaker on top of the helmet, keeping it in place. On the heel—Jonas saw them all earlier, pretended to just be counting tiles in the floor—is the number 42 in black marker. Geoff Koenig's number.

Behind that white shoe, there's seven others. Ninth-grader feet. Girl shoes.

Shelly Graham, Michael's big sister, asks Jonas where's he going here? There a rifle hid back in one of these lockers, maybe?

She fakes looking around for a police officer.

Jonas pulls on his helmet again, no luck.

Another of the ninth graders standing there is Ginger Koenig, her eyes twin tunnels of eyeliner.

She's breathing hard here.

Jonas doesn't know what to say to her, or how to say it, so he just opens his mouth, says her name like a question.

It's enough.

Her right shoe comes down on his wrist, hard enough to make it roll sideways, palm up.

Jonas tries to pull his arm to him, can't, and is about to start making some noise about this when there's a pair of heels clacking back past the water fountains, saying something stern that ends in a question mark but isn't a question at all. A teacher. Ms. Marugg.

Ginger Koenig's shoe steps away, the four girls forming a fast wall, the helmet already under Shelly Graham's arm somehow, like it's been there all along, and by then Jonas is rolling back into the darkness, flattening himself in the shallow entry of a supply closet.

Behind him, Ms. Marugg steps on the bottom lip of the aluminum gate, the lock catching with a dull, permanent thunk.

Then nothing. Just Jonas, there.

Crying at last but not too loud.

He tries to push the tears back in with the heels of his hands. Tries pinching his thighs, then hitting them with the side of his fists. Finally just steps out and runs through the halls, the carpet hiding his footsteps.

This is the night he steps into the teacher's lounge, looks around, pees in the metal trash can. He calls it vindication, never tells anybody.

Because all the doors to outside are locked, he has to cut through the visiting team's locker room to the practice gym, then from there through the coaches' offices, and out onto the floor of the main gym where the players enter.

He keeps his head down, walks a straight line to the visitor side of the gym, stepping sideways through the kneeling cheerleaders, and slips up through the blue-pipe rails before anybody can say anything, then he's running again, through the cafeteria, out into the parking lot, across to the field house.

His helmet's already there, hanging off the throttle grip like the helmet in a movie.

Nothing done to it either, not even perfume, or ketchup, or the stubby little glitter pens all the girls are dangling from their wrists that year.

Jonas nods to himself that this is okay then.

That it wasn't so bad.

He screws the spark plug back in through whatever grit's on the threads, from his pocket probably, plants his feet on the pegs and rips the cord up into the sky.

The three-wheeler starts at once and he revs it too high, a message to everybody in the gym, but then it sputters out, won't start from the cord anymore.

The plug. That has to be it.

Jonas checks it, making sure the wire hasn't come off, then breaks it over with the little wrench, pulls it out to check the contact, see if it got bent shut when he was rolling under the gate.

But then he tastes the problem on the air.

Like his dad's tea when they go to town to eat.

Under the three-wheeler, still fluttering away, pink sweetener packets, all the corners torn off perfectly, the way a girl would do it.

The Sweet 'N Low's not just in the tank either, like could be siphoned out maybe, then flushed. It's been poured in through the spark plug hole he left gaping.

It's what the grit was.

He sticks his finger in, takes it back out. Cleans it in the dirt and then keeps cleaning it.

When the game's over thirty minutes later, Jonas is waiting in the passenger seat of Earl Holbrook's truck. Earl Holbrook studies him, like he's trying to make sense of who this could be. Finally he climbs in anyway, no questions, the helmet on the seat between them leaning his way until Jonas catches it, pulls it back.

"Where's Sissy?" Jonas says. It's the only adult thing he can think of. Ten minutes ago she was silhouetted in the double doors, the man with the phone in his briefcase standing just behind her, watching her.

Earl just sits there, his hands on the wheel, his face pale. Blinking too much, it seems. Or, not too much, but in clumps, all at once.

"What?" Jonas says, tasting the air again, this time for smoke.

That's not it, though.

But it kind of is, too.

Earl Holbrook laughs a sick little laugh to himself, a bad sound, and says it like the punch line of a joke, almost, something he's just reciting to himself: "Her niece, Stacy, she died last night. They just…just—"

Ten minutes later, his truck turns left back onto Cloverdale instead of right, the direction he lives.

"Where's he going?" Jonas says to his mom.

They're at the door.

Belinda's crying too, just heard about it over the phone.

"Home," she says, "he's going home," then pushes away, runs to her room so that, when Rob King finally comes in, Jonas is feeding his brothers cartoon cereal with too much milk. At eleven o'clock, a black-and-white horror movie on the television.

"So where's that death machine, then?" Rob says, using Belinda's term for the three-wheeler, hanging his hat on the hook above the washer but moving slow too, like he doesn't want to miss whatever Jonas' answer might be here.

Jonas doesn't have one, though.

"Where's your mom?" Rob King says next, quieter, scanning the empty living room, and Jonas just looks out the window by the table, doesn't have an answer for this either.

If he can get exactly four Honeycombs in each of his next three spoonfuls, though, then everything will be all right.

It matters.

***

A word about Hot Wheels.

A book about them, really.

The die-cast line of toy cars was born in 1968. And those first ones, they weren't the same size as the ones we all know. The ones we all know are 1:43. In 1968, they were 1:64. That first year there were sixteen of them, just to test the market, see if boys would really be into these things—if there was enough room on the shelves for Matchbox *and* Hot Wheels.

There was.

There is.

Today, there's some ten thousand different models in circulation.

These little cars, I mean, they never die.

All of the spirals and notebooks I used to carry in second grade, sure, there'd be KISS stickers on front—Barry Gibb, too, cut out from a record sleeve, the light hazy behind his hair—but the pages, they were littered with my designs. I was going to revolutionize the market for this toy. Make it not a toy at all, but a little reproduction. It would have real air conditioner ductwork, the hood on the Bandit-edition Trans-Am would open the right way, there'd be removable T-tops, pinstriping so fine it would have to have been drawn with a single hair, and then another traced right beside it, impossibly close.

This was the year we were living in town, on Roosevelt.

There were only so many hours of daylight after school (Midland Christian, the first failed experiment), but my brother and me, we were working in a scale so small—1:43—that there would be weeks between three-thirty and dinner, generations of stories to untangle, drive our way out of. And if we couldn't go outside, then the kitchen had linoleum, and we'd stage elaborate demolitions, one car at a time, marveling after each crash how all that ever happened was chipped paint, sometimes a wheel angled up into the well.

How we carried the little cars was a white five-gallon bucket.

And if you want to know about the first betrayal I can remember, it's coming home on a Saturday from somewhere, my brother out front with the bucket. There were more cars now, so it was overflowing into the grass. And he was trying not to smile.

What had happened: he'd been buying the little cars one at a time all morning, from kids up and down the block. What he'd been paying for the cars with was my collection of 1972 silver dollars. Every birthday, Christmas and special day, I'd been getting one of them.

This is when I stopped playing little cars.

After that, what we used the bucket for was horny toads. Even in town, they were everywhere. You couldn't hit an empty lot without stepping on one. Give us one morning, and my brother and me could fill that five-gallon bucket to the wire handle with horny toads, so that when our mom made us pour them out at the end of the day, the bottom third would usually be soggy, flat, and dead.

It didn't matter. There were more. And we knew them all, could tell the males from the females (spots), knew the drag race ones from the slowbies (light green under the armpit), knew how to tell when one was pregnant (the tail), and could even get them to spit blood from their eyes on command (Clayton next door's yellow lab). I remember once even dragging my mom all the way down the block, so she could see a rare event: a horny toad giving birth. It was one of the big ones that fill your whole hand, their side armor poking your palm so you have to really want to hold on.

My mom—this was in an abandoned carport—so willing to step into that hot shade, but already holding the back of her hand to her mouth as well. Her nose.

What I thought was the miracle of birth was maggots boiling up from the split belly of the horny toad.

My mom laughed and cried at the same time, kind of, and carried me away, even when I fought to go back, watch some more.

Ten years later, moving pipe back in Greenwood, where there should really *be* horny toads, big ones like you used to see in aquariums in doctor's offices, I only clearly remember seeing one. It had spent the night close to the aluminum pipe because the pipe had soaked up all of yesterday's heat, I think. When I lifted the pipe, the horny toad just looked up at me, craning its head, its horns almost touching its back.

"Hey, you," I said to it, still balancing the pipe, ready to walk it twelve rows forward, shift it in with the last until the latch caught.

The horny toad just looked up at me.

"Don't worry," I told it, "I'm different now."

At six-thirty in the morning you talk to everything.

It just kept staring up at me.

I nodded bye to it, set the pipe then came back for the next, and the next, and, maybe four joints later, finally remembered that horny toad.

Out in the dirt like that, exposed, it was hawk food. I guessed a hawk would eat one, anyway.

So I went back, couldn't find it, was finally forced to go footprint by footprint in the wet dirt, my keys out so I could drop them if I heard a truck, say they were what I'd been looking for.

Then there it was, flattened under one of my heels, driven deep because I'd been carrying fifty pounds of pipe.

I didn't say anything to it.

It was one of the fast ones, too. It could have run.

I was by the Phillips place then, and didn't have time for this kind of stuff, but did it anyway: buried that horny toad up in the pasture, the burial ground, in a hole I had to kick with my heel.

There would be more, and more.

And I'm lying again, can't help it.

That with the cars, it wasn't my first betrayal.

The first was in that square little white house I don't remember, I think. It's the only one that sort of matches, anyway. I'm maybe three here, could be four. In the kitchen on my knees, building a flat pyramid of blocks, the kind with letters all over them.

It's taken me all morning.

The reason I've had all morning: my mom and dad have been screaming up and down the hall, into the living room. Doors slamming, brushes flying into walls, the dogs outside putting up a wall of sound.

This is back when it used to be like that. It was something about whose fault it was. How it had changed everything. How it didn't—they'd just been *kids*, for God's sake. *Kids*.

Or, that's what I have them say now, anyway. What fits.

I don't know, though. Back then it was just noise.

And then it draws near, all at once: my mom at the living-room doorway of the kitchen, her face a mess, my dad at the other doorway, the one that opens onto the hall.

I'm perfectly between them.

My mom says my dad's name in a new way, and I look up to him, have to crane my neck to do it.

What he does here is smile. Blow something like a laugh out his nose, but not. Definitely not.

What he does here is step forward once, twice, and on the third step, his boot crashes directly through my pyramid, kicks through so the blocks explode all over the kitchen, letters on the counter, in the sink, my mom covering her face from them but reaching for me too.

It's the kind of dramatic he wants, and that's where that scene cuts off sharp.

That same year, though, another picks up: I'm with my Uncle Jackson. He's picked me up from the house, let me stand in the seat of his truck beside him, is taking me nowhere particular. Just away.

It's perfect.

Finally we end up at this road over towards Stanton that's blacktop now but was dirt then. His friends are there—he's still in high school, has these velvety skeleton posters in his room that terrify me—and they're all racing their cars.

I have about four seconds of this, total.

It's enough.

I'm standing behind the two cars set up to go next, and then their tires start spinning and the world goes brown and loud, and the only thing I can hold onto is my uncle's hand.

It's the least scared I've ever been.

***

Because Stacy Monahans' funeral's just in Lamesa, nobody from Greenwood starts heading that way until after lunch.

As for the investigation—investigations—there's been zero progress: any one of a hundred made-up people could have started the fire, for any of a thousand reasons, though there's still the rumor that the police have a bagful of guilty cigarette butts, and, though shooting into a moving bus is a very punishable crime, the Sheriff's office finally has no slug to match with any shot-through medals, no gun to get more slugs from, and, aside from that, no real motive.

What they've tried to make stick, indirectly—they don't say this in Belinda King's living room, but still, people know—is that it was mostly King cotton that burned, and it was one King in specific who got a hospital wristband on his *other* wrist; Rob King's first surgery is scheduled for the second week in February.

And if the pumper Steve Grimes didn't start the fires, just for general mischief, then yeah, who else could have but the offseason basketball players? As a joke, maybe. Their way of telling Fidel to kiss it, that they hated this running through the cotton bullshit.

Or, at the end of December, right after Grimes was cleared, that was the thinking anyway.

Geoff Koenig getting shot changed all of that, though.

Now the basketball team was holy, the underdog, had never done anything wrong. Won even when they lost, just because they *played*.

If Geoff had been killed, though? If that animated bullet had slapped him in the temple instead of the shoulder?

Yeah.

The thinking at the Sheriff's office, which had been at some point *out-loud* thinking, was that if Geoff Koenig had been shot like that, then the shooter, his misguided revenge would have been complete, right?

One of the players who had put the things in motion that got this shooter's dad hurt, that player would have paid.

Jonas hadn't gone back for the rest of the tournament, no.

Where he was, mostly, was in his dad's shop.

The lesson he was learning was engine maintenance.

Instead of using a manual to take his little 110 motor apart, put it back together, his dad was making him do it by trial and error. At the end of the day, when it wouldn't start again, his dad would lick his lips, nod, and ask Jonas if he'd scraped this gasket all the way flat, or if he'd made sure that valve was clean before tapping it back into place.

The first day the job had smelled like sweet tea.

Now it just tasted like hate.

For Shelly Graham. For Ginger Koenig, and for Melissa Simms, who'd been part of it too, and for Geoff himself, for sitting in that bus seat like an idiot. Leonard, for being in that part of the road at that bad moment. Coach Harrison, for thinking they even had a chance at that tournament without Tommy Moore to rain his special brand of fire down on Iraan and the rest of them.

Hate for Tommy Moore, for not fighting back.

This one Jonas dwelled on, was already preparing for in his head: some rough-handed farmer pulling *him* off a bale someday, and how he, Jonas, wasn't going to just ball up like Tommy Moore.

Jonas was going to come off that bale swinging, until the deputies have to pull *him* off of Rob King.

Or whoever.

But all sons think this, yeah. Dream it. Never do it.

Another scene: this kid is sitting on his dad's shoulders. He's five or so. They're walking down the packed-dirt driveway of the house where the dad grew up. Just going down to the road for some reason, when, before the sound even, the thunder that rattles their teeth, there's this sudden spike of light standing in the ground past the fence from them, just across Cloverdale, maybe on it, even.

The kid's looking right into it, too.

A dome of color swells up where it hits, holds for a flash, burns itself into his head, and then they're running, the kid's dad pulling him down into his arms so they won't be so tall, and the kid, the whole time they're running he's just bouncing in his dad's arms, and looking behind them, around his dad, at the flash. Thinking what if they'd already been down there.

Not quite eight years later, head swimming with comic panels, this kid will stand out on the concrete block porch of the house they're living in, the one his grandfather's letting them use until they find their feet again, moneywise.

What the kid's out there for is the storm, the sky pulsing with light, the horses screaming back in the pens.

And he's wet, and it's cold, and his mom's calling his name from inside, but instead of answering he just reaches higher up into the sky with the chrome car antenna he's been saving, and this kid, what he's doing is waiting to become somebody else.

By the time that happens, he'll have pretty much forgotten who he'd ever been in the first place.

It won't mean 1985 and 1986 never happened, though.

Just that they didn't have to.

Chapter Nine

This is what Larry Monahans will tell you, if you can ever get up the nerve to call him:

- that it's funny hearing from you, after all this time
- that—what's it run a person to hunt up there?
- that he hates talking on the phone like this
- that no, he doesn't read much
- that he doesn't do much rocket science either
- that—what's this bullshit about 'Monahans?' Some kind of *joke*?

What he won't say, ever:

- that it was his irrigation spillover Stacy hydroplaned on that night
- that it was two hours before he got to a phone to call in about her
- that maybe that's why he hates carry-phones—for what they didn't do for him that morning
- that, still, he was maybe the fourth person in Dawson County to get one installed in his truck that year.

What you know but won't have the nerve to ask:

- that before the insurance adjustor could get there the following week, Larry Monahans had already scraped a ditch as deep into the earth as his backhoe could reach, and then, using the back of that yellow shovel like a huge wrist, nudged a Subaru he didn't have title to over into the ditch, packed the dirt back in over it
- that the insurance adjustor was convinced to write his report all the same
- that Daniel Gonzales, who had owned that Subaru, got a sudden urge to move in early 1986, before school was over, never mind that, according to the yearbook, track was his sport
- that Daniel Gonzales' uncle caught that urge to move as well
- that a lot of Mexicans maybe did
- that Larry Monahans still farms that same field Stacy died in, won't let it rest even for a year
- that it's the cleanest field in the county
- that Gwen, in 1986, she'd just been waiting for Stacy to graduate, so she could pack her bags
- that she's still waiting.

What you'll hear yourself saying, and cringe from:

- that—is that burger place still there right when you come into town? Old red and white one?
- that yeah, you know the Sky-Vue. You saw *Footloose* there once, a family tr—
- that Wednesday'll work, sure
- that—that the laughter is what you'll remember, when you remember the way that it was.

That last part'll just be in your head, though. It's been there for more than half your life already, is sometimes the only piece of verse you can remember.

As for who wrote it, maybe Gwen Monahans would know. It's from the program for her daughter's funeral. The script everybody got handed at the gate, so they'd know what to do, when to do it.

It didn't help.

***

The morning of the funeral, Jonas is standing in the doorway of Rob King's shop, watching Earl Holbrook ease past what used to be their pump house, his truck stepping up onto the CRP grass like a horse with tender hooves, testing every step.

Earl's arm is out the window, his nice jacket already on. The passenger seat's empty, a black dress for Sissy hanging from his gun rack in her place because she's been in Lamesa since the first night of the tournament.

When Earl first nosed his truck up their road, Jonas had stepped out to meet him, to jump in back—Earl had to be there to fix the basketball goal, finally—but Belinda rapped on the kitchen window, shook her head no.

Because Jonas had already promised not to get his good pants dirty before the funeral—not to make this day any worse than it already was—he'd slouched back to his cinderblock in the shop, stared at his three-wheeler's stupid, stupid engine, exploding the diagram of it in his head, trying to make sure he hadn't forgotten some vital step, some essential part.

He knows better than to touch it with anything but memory, though.

Inside, his brothers are suffering the blow dryer, getting lectures about proper behavior.

Jonas almost has to smile about that.

"She make you promise too?" Rob King asks, suddenly in the shop.

"He need help?" Jonas tilts his head to the back of the section. To Earl Holbrook.

Rob King focuses out there, shrugs. "He'll be all right," he says. "And don't think you're getting out of riding with us up there."

Rob King smooths his grin down.

"How far is it?" Jonas asks.

"What?"

"To Lamesa."

"Hour. Not even."

"So we'll be back before dark?"

"You want to ride it again, don't you?" Rob King says.

Jonas shrugs. He wants to ride that 110 faster than anybody's ever gone, yeah. But he doesn't say it.

Rob King's suit jacket, it's draped over his slinged arm.

"Did you know her?" Jonas says then, reaching out as if to touch the Honda's plug wire, the last piece he snugged back on, because that was where it all started. You have to remember those kinds of things.

"Who?"

"Stacy. The Monahans girl."

Rob King studies Jonas hard.

"You know to be careful on water like that, right?" he finally says. "You can't trust it."

"Her car was too light," Jonas repeats. It's what everybody's been saying about the wreck.

"She was your cousin," Rob King says, looking back to Earl Holbrook again. "Second, I guess."

"It was like this for Uncle Sterling?" Jonas says then, pure ambush. "When he…you know?"

Pure ambush if he'd actually said it, I mean.

Rob King reaches across to the bench grinder, spins the stone wheel.

"Yeah," he says, or would have, watching the wheel slow, "yeah, it was just like this, pretty much."

Lies. All of it.

***

This is piecemeal, secondhand, polluted, cleaned-up then tore down, worse, but still, it's the only way it could have gone, too. The way it had to have been.

The morning the wrecker delivered Sterling King's truck back to Arthur King's house, deposited it back by the silver fuel tanks for some reason, like that's all it needed, another tank of gas, Arthur King and his wife didn't even know the wrecker had been there.

It was November, stripping season, so Arthur King hadn't been home that night to get the phone call.

Like his nephew an hour north and years and years later, Arthur King would be one of the first in his county to get a phone wired into the dash of his main truck.

That's all after the fact, though, after he woke one morning to smoke in the air, bellowed back inside for his wife to call the fire station, to call them all; after everything could have gone different, maybe, if she had called, let somebody in a fireproof jacket be the one to find Tommy Moore up on that module.

But it wasn't her fault, either, what Rob King had done to Tommy Moore that morning.

The best part of her had died seventeen years before with the phone call from Odessa. She hadn't even been able to call the rest of her kids, all so many years younger than Sterling. She couldn't even make her way out to the turnrow of whatever field Arthur was in, flash him down with her headlights.

In 1968, Arthur's mother was still alive, too. Living with them. Pushing her wooden walker from room to room, a chamber pot under her bed because that's the way she still remembered things being.

Days, she was generally okay, but during the night she wandered, scraping her walker's legs across the floor. It had gotten regular enough that Arthur had tacked down the curls in the linoleum where it met the carpet so she wouldn't topple over.

The night Sterling died, she scraped all the way back into the closet of the master bedroom.

It was where Cecilia King was hiding after the phone call. After the news. She had crawled back behind the dresses she cycled through each Sunday, a cycle twenty-two deep now, so deep that nobody could even claim it was a cycle, really. But Cecilia knew, kept careful count.

When her mother-in-law found her, Cecilia had the doubled-over hem of one of her twenty-two dresses in her mouth, was trying to swallow it.

And you can't think bad of her for that, please.

I remember in a department store once, during the Gulf War, a woman, obviously a mom, getting a call on her bulky cell phone, and then falling to the ground by the escalator but running with her feet at the same time so she was just pushing around on the tile floor, the phone still pressed to the side of her head, a sound coming from her mouth I don't want to ever hear again.

Nobody knew what to do with her either.

But Mrs. King, with her daughter-in-law, she tried, held out the only thing she had, the main thing.

Mouse's medals.

Over the years, Cecilia King would come to think they'd been her son's. That Mouse and Sterling were the same person, somehow.

And they kind of were, I guess.

But she couldn't tell anybody.

Rob King, though.

He had to have, at some point.

None of this makes sense otherwise.

And the truck, the one the wrecker delivered.

When Arthur King got back from being on the stripper all night, because Sterling had never shown up for his shift, he saw Sterling's truck back there by the tanks, and coasted past the house. Just to ask, as calmly as he could manage, What the *hell*, son?

Except then Sterling wasn't in the truck.

And the truck's back window, it was mostly gone.

There are certain rear bumpers a person should never *have* to step up onto, so they can see into a bed.

Or, no: there are certain bumpers some people *should* have to step up onto, so that they can look down on this bed they've made.

Arthur King screws three garden hoses together, his hands shaking around the brass connectors so it takes longer than it should, then lowers the tailgate of the truck, sprays what's in there out and keeps spraying, the mist all around him rising in a cloud.

An hour later he goes into his house by the back door, leaves his boots by the mat and walks through the house, finally finds his mother.

She's on the train track rug in the boys' room, the two youngest sleeping in their twin beds, the other one suddenly standing in the doorway in his underwear and a t-shirt, bleary-eyed.

"Dad?" he says.

This is Robert.

"Go to sleep," Arthur tells him, "it's too early," and guides him back.

It takes him another half hour to locate his wife.

She's in the garage now, back in the corner.

"Cecilia," he says, holding a hand out for her, and she comes out too fast for him to stop, is hitting him in the chest over and over with the sides of her fists.

He raises his chin, closes his eyes, wishes with all earnestness that she wasn't so frail.

***

Telephones.

This isn't a book about Hot Wheels, but a book about calling people.

The phone rings at ten minutes past eleven, fifty minutes before Rob King's said they have to leave to pay their respects. The call shakes the whole shop, it feels like, so that Jonas jumps. It has to be loud, though, if Rob's going to hear it when he's working.

In a novel, Jonas would find a way to listen in, or would step out onto the apron of concrete in front of the shop, so that at the same time he could see his dad, leaning against the metal wall by his workbench, and his mom in the kitchen, listening in, and read the conversation by their faces.

I wish.

Instead, Jonas' father hangs the phone up gently, the hand he was holding it with gloved because he wasn't able to stop spinning that grinder wheel.

He bites the glove off, drops it onto the bench. Spits the grit from his tongue, that black taste you always tell yourself to remember's going to happen.

"What?" Jonas says, ready for some reason to run again. To get his brothers somehow, in the red wagon maybe, and just take off through the grass.

Rob King doesn't answer, just shakes his head like he should have known.

On the way through the door he clamps his left hand onto Jonas' shoulder, pulls him along, to the house.

Jonas shrugs his shoulder away, but follows.

Belinda's waiting for him in the kitchen, a white pen between her fingers that at first looks like a cigarette.

"Who was it?" she says.

Rob King looks around like it's not the kind of thing just anybody can be hearing.

"It's okay, Dad," Jonas says, angling his eyes hard to his mom, for support.

"What?" she says again to Rob.

"Pete," he says. Just that.

Belinda stares at him, and the way she's doing it, this is an old fight. One they don't have time for right now.

Not in front of Jonas, anyway.

"Mr. Manson?" Jonas says.

"Peter Rabbit," Rob King says, his eyes on Belinda the whole time.

"Goddammit," Belinda says then, and Jonas feels the blood all wash from his face.

Not because in Sunday school he's been taught, and absolutely believes, that taking the Lord's name in vain is the worst of the bad—his mind filling the moment the teacher said that, filling with profanity he didn't even know he had—but because this word, this swear, it's coming from his mom.

Rob King, though, he smiles, hearing it. Like now things are getting interesting.

"That was Dwayne Jenkins," he says, hitting each syllable, each letter. "Deputy?"

"The one you hit, yeah."

Rob King shrugs like that's nothing, is already gone. That maybe they've been hitting each other as hard as they could since fourth grade or so. Doesn't mean a thing.

"I'm not going to play this," Belinda says, scooping her earrings from the marble ashtray by the phone, angling her head over for them.

"You don't have to," Rob says, "not anymore."

This doesn't stop her forcing her earrings home, but it does settle her eyes on him.

"Joney," she says to Jonas, lifting her eyebrows to the back of the house. To his brothers, maybe. That this is where he leaves the room.

"But, Mom—"

"*But nothing,*" Rob says, not ever looking over at Jonas.

Jonas sulks out, down the hall. Slams his door.

Though he can't see his parents anymore now, still, his hand to the knob so he can scoot in if he needs to, dive for his bed, he hears enough:

Belinda: What do you mean we don't have to anymore?

Rob: I mean maybe it wasn't . . .

Probably a head nod here. Down the hall at a certain closed door.

Belinda: He already told us he didn't do it.

Rob: Yeah, well. Telling's one thing, this is another.

Belinda: Who, then?

Some crude pantomime of a gut, a belly, maybe.

Belinda, hushing her voice: Pete?

Most likely a smile here.

No, a grin. A slow grin, Rob King milking the moment. Like he's been waiting for it for years.

And who knows.

As for the rest, this isn't all from what they say in the kitchen before the funeral that day, but that's just because they didn't have to say it all, already knew most of it.

Pete Manson.

Without physical evidence, the Sheriff's office had fallen back to financials, to see if that would supply something along the lines of motive for the arson.

Bingo.

Pete Manson was going under, pretty much the same way cartoon cats drowned: holding his hand up once, somebody save me; twice, help; then the third time: later, dudes.

And, just as important, though Arthur King had lost twenty modules to the fire, there'd been two strips of land leased there as well, with five modules packed down at the end of the turnrows.

Two of them were Earl Holbrook's, his only plot. He was either trying to get a toe-hold back into farming or he was farming just enough that he could still run farm tags on his trucks. Or just because it was in his blood, these plants.

That's just twenty-two of the modules, though.

The other three? Pete Manson's.

The idea—this was all later—was that he'd started setting his planters with odd skips in them so that, everything else being the same, Rooster might opt to just go ahead and let him lease those strips of land again, seeing as how they already had his signature rows up and down them. It was a way of holding on, of grubbing for just one more year.

But—burn his *own* crop?

This is key.

Once you've packed your module and pulled the builder off it and called the gin for your number to spraypaint on the end, it's insured by the gin. If it rains before the driver gets there, it's their fault, and the gin pays out. But there's some grey area there, too: if the module *collapses* before the gin's truck gets there, then that's your fault—you didn't pack it tight enough. Or, in Pete's case, you'd packed it with a module builder seeping hydraulic fluid from every piston, a module builder with walls that weren't Death Star at all, that were leaving loose, crumbly modules.

Even back then, Pete was gambling, yeah.

But he was smart, too. He'd talked his agent into letting him pay a bit extra for a month or two, to put some insurance on top of what the gin would cover. And they did it without inspecting his module builder, even. And, better yet, if something happened to these modules, not only would the gin pay out—and, for fire, they would—but his side-insurance would as well, and at last year's price per bale, which had been the highest in years.

So there was motive, yeah. Where there's money, there's motive. The clincher was the two cigarette butts the Sheriff was finally letting out of the evidence locker.

They were Chesterfields. Pete's brand. Documented as his when he crushed one out in the road the day of the shooting, when he was looking for the magic bullet. When he crushed one out and the Sheriff stepped over, kept his boot on it until Pete was back in the ditch.

Maybe inconsequential, considering Pete Manson was working those fields, had been giving Arthur King a hand when needed, and everybody knew he smoked, left his butts behind him like bread crumbs. However, add to this the insurance motive, how that insurance could float his farm another year, and then add to *that* that he was the first truck on the scene the day of the fire, and, well.

It might be for a jury to decide. For some Midland lawyer, fresh from tennis with Martin Ledbetter, to shrug and present the facts with all due reluctance, like he's just saying what these fine, sequestered people are already thinking: that, when Pete Manson pulled Rob King off poor Tommy Moore that fateful morning, a very decisive act, mind, a very decisive act from a man usually content to watch whatever goings-on he's presented with, that—how could he have *been* so decisive, how could he have been so *certain* Rob King was beating the wrong boy, right?

Unless of course he knew something everybody else didn't.

***

This still isn't the funeral, either.

But we're getting there.

The house, Rob and Belinda King's cul-de-sac cut into the middle of a field of what had been CRP. That stands for Conservation Reserve Program. Probably something I should have said way earlier, yeah.

This isn't my native mode, though, non-fiction.

Each page, I want to quit.

To keep the names and dates straight—properly crooked—it's taken sheets and sheets of scratch paper.

A reader not from Greenwood, reading this, maybe it'll make some kind of sense, won't feel like trying to hold too many marbles in your hand.

Somebody who was there, though: I'm sorry.

All the names you know, they're attached to the wrong people. They're hiding the right people.

Rocket science, yeah.

But we're almost there, now.

What you need to do here is picture Jonas in that hall, that morning before the funeral. His hand is still to the knob, his white shirt hanging on the other side of that door, and probably buttoned up besides.

He's prepared for the trouble he's going to be in, too, when he has to push the door open, dive for the bed, unroll a comic book so it's almost to the end.

He just forgot to put his shirt on, Mom, okay?

If he's smart, what he would add there is a "goddammit," to deflect her suspicion—*direct* her anger.

If he could even say that word, I mean.

Instead, he's likely to say he was just thinking about Stacy Monahans. From the reunion that time, when the Kings used to have them down at the Greenwood Elementary, and the men would bring shoes for the basketball court and the women would sit in the cafeteria talking, the smaller kids underfoot, the older ones running through the whole school exactly like they own it. Larry Monahans just standing in the entry with his cousins, the three of them sharing a red cup to spit in.

That first reunion she's at—the only—she's twelve, about, Stacy.

It's the first year for them and the Holbrooks both.

But Earl, instead of talking to his brother-in-law in the entry, he's in the gym, lobbing flat balls at the basket. Looking for a broom to get the ones down that stay up there, wedged against the back of the rim and the backboard. Jonas there too, sailing shots from the free-throw line, about as far as he can shoot from.

And, I say it's the first year they made the trip, but of course there's more to it than the hour drive.

Just as Arthur King, once upon a time, had quietly absorbed his brother Mouse's quarter of the land, thereby doubling his own, so had he reabsorbed the land that had been intended for Sterling.

Except, unlike Mouse, Sterling had left a couple of kids that would have been in that line of inheritance.

Never mind that Sterling's widow Macinaw—a name I've never heard again, and maybe just some version or mishearing of her birth certificate name—that she was already married to a farmer up in Lamesa. That her kids were taking *his* name now.

But they were still Kings. Even if they wouldn't understand what that meant for another year or two.

It hit Sissy different than it hit Larry, yeah. Hit him over and over and over, until he started hitting back.

So, there was that.

But, here they are too, at the reunion for the first time. One a farmer himself, the kind who doesn't smile a lot or ever take his hat off, the other a farmer's wife, that one even living back in Greenwood, since her husband had put down roots in high school.

The girl who would have been Sterling King's first grandchild standing on her toes at the water fountain, trying to keep her face dry. Stacy Monahans.

It's the main memory Jonas has of her, of her trying to reach that sputtering arc of water. It's what he plans to maybe use if Belinda goes into a rage about his shirt still being on the door.

He never has to, though.

Just when his parents' voices are starting to get loud and lower at the same time, his brother opens the bathroom door behind him, and—this is all so fast—wails it down the hall: "Mo-om!"

Belinda King is there in an instant, Jonas' hand still to the knob, him figuring out he's caught, her understanding that he's been listening in, when Rob King says it, from somewhere Jonas can't see: *"Lin."*

It's the tone that turns her around.

Jonas follows.

His dad is at the kitchen window. Belinda now too.

Jonas doesn't have to go that far, can see through the sliding glass door fine.

It's the Sheriff. Just sitting there in his car.

Rob King steps onto the back porch and Jonas is about to follow when Belinda stops him, her hand on his shoulder, like pulling him out of a fast road.

"But—" Jonas tries.

Belinda doesn't let him go.

Rob King takes his time making it out there, turning his face to Cloverdale for a moment, maybe to track a truck, heading east to cut north too, like they need to be doing as well. A couple sitting on either side of that bench seat, uncomfortable in their clothes, a covered dish between them.

Because the Sheriff doesn't stand from his car—he's the only one in it—Rob King has to lean down to the window, his loose jacket like a cape in the wind.

In answer to whatever the Sheriff's asking, Rob looks all around, shakes his head, and the Sheriff stares straight ahead, like he expected no less here.

He's not stupid either, though.

He tips the brim of his hat up, then, with that same hand, reaches out the window, waves Jonas over.

Jonas steps back, now.

"Mom?"

Rob King stands, looks over as well. Leans over to spit but never drops his eyes.

"Mom?" Jonas says again, holding her wrist now, keeping her hand on his shoulder, but Rob King nods, his eyes telling her something Jonas can't crack into. It gets her to slide the door back.

"It'll be all right," she says, taking her hand back, but Jonas can hear the waver in her voice.

"Go," she says to him when he looks up to be sure, so he does, stiff-legging it out across the packed dirt, past the blown-up pump house, all the way to the Sheriff's car. Just finds himself there all at once.

"Looking for somebody, son," the Sheriff says, like last time never happened.

"I already told you—" Rob starts, but the Sheriff stops him with "I'm asking the *boy*, Mr. King."

Rob King bites his lower lip gently, raises both his hands, the good one and the broke one.

"Ask," he says. "Same answer."

The Sheriff smiles to himself, says, "I don't doubt that," then, to Jonas: "Mr. Holbrook. Earlybird Earl. Seen him today?"

What he's doing is covering his bases. I know that now.

Earl Holbrook lost two modules in the fire. *Un*insured, because he hadn't called the gin for his number yet—of all people, it was the gin manager who took too long to get his module logged in. The Sheriff's office can't have it looking like they were just targeting Pete Manson. It has to look like Pete Manson distinguished himself from the suspect pool all by himself. For reasons the jury will find all too obvious.

Jonas, though—this is all a mystery to him.

"Uncle Earl?" he says, stalling, squinting too much, overplaying, like he's having to struggle to even connect the name to a face here.

"Friend of the family, I believe," the Sheriff adds, nothing but a smile in his voice. "Seen him around these parts today?"

More than anything in the world, Jonas wants to look up to his dad, see the answer he needs to give, but this is the principal's office, and sometimes you just have to throw an answer out there, make it right in the way you say it.

"Son?" the Sheriff adds.

"He's not your—" Rob King starts, the Sheriff cutting his eyes to him fast now, a warning Rob's not backing down from anymore, and this more than anything, the way it's going to end again if Rob King says anything else, this gets Jonas to finally say it: "He hasn't been here all day."

"Earl Holbrook hasn't been here all day?"

Jonas nods that that's correct, yes.

"See?" Rob King says.

The Sheriff smiles again, so tolerant, and lowers his cruiser into reverse. "Guess I got some bad information then," he says, and nods his farewell, leaves Rob and Jonas King standing there behind him, Jonas already craning back across the grass, for Earl Holbrook.

Rob King, his hand to Jonas' shoulder, guides his face back to the road, to Cloverdale.

Instead of turning right, back towards Midland, his office, the Sheriff brakes at the cattle guard and holds it, holds it, then finally turns left, the direction the trucks have been going all day.

Lamesa.

"Shit," Rob King says, and doesn't even tell Jonas not to repeat that word around his mother.

Jonas doesn't anyway.

Not yet.

***

Because everybody from Greenwood cuts up 137 to get to Stacy Monahan's funeral, none of them have to drive by the field on 349 she died in. The only reason she was on it instead of 137 is that she wasn't going to Greenwood that night, but Midland, where Geoff Koenig had checked back in with a fever. Specifically, Midland Memorial Hospital, the place the doctors killed my brother's son, the place I had to go in the third grade to have my tongue sewed back on, the place I went the first and second times I broke my hand, the first place that sewed my Achilles back together. The place we'd all been born. The place my mom had a head-on collision, so that the nurses just had to wheel a gurney out to the street.

She was okay, had been thinking about something else, had no explanation for drifting over to the wrong side of the road.

I didn't come down from Lubbock that time. Everybody told me I didn't have to, that it was just her truck that was hurt, but that's not why I listened to them, I don't think. When I was five, maybe, still riding in the passenger side floorboard, the one with a hole rusted in the bottom, she'd wrecked too, in Big Springs, and, what I remember is rolling forward in that floorboard over and over and over, somebody finally lifting me up from there so that I could stop rolling.

I don't know.

The firemen thought I was broken, probably. Head trauma, repetitive motion. Everything else.

I was just being safe, though.

My mom was okay that time too, and all the rest.

And nobody rolls their truck over getting to this funeral, their covered dish floating right beside their head for some impossible moment.

Rob King even stops in Stanton, pulls his super cab up into the cinder block stall of the two-hole carwash, blows the grime off, Belinda and Jonas and his two brothers sitting inside, hundreds of pounds of water pressure hitting the glass from all sides.

"Little gentlemen," Belinda says.

They all know.

When Rob gets back in, he's mostly dry.

In Stanton, in 1986, the big MOTEL sign is still looming up on the other side of the road, a sign Jonas never understood, like it's some artifact left over from when Stanton had been this huge, bright place. Except he knows it never was, will even sneak into the nine rooms of the broke-down motel years later, after the sign's gone, to see if there's an explanation in there, in the drawers, the rat-nest tubs. There won't be. The only leftover, really, will be the giant concrete blocks that the sign had been set in. He'll stand there between them, look up.

Generations of Buffaloes probably climbed it. Looked all around, the whole town there below them—three thousand people and a few old soreheads, according to the sign on the highway. They'd looked all around and wished they hadn't climbed up there, didn't have to see.

Sometimes it's better to be the ant.

Because there's no dryer at the carwash, Rob King punches the accelerator until Belinda says it without turning around: "Seatbelts."

There's only one that's not lost under the shallow backseat, though.

Jonas clicks it closed three times, so they won't have to make any more stops, and his brother's eyes widen. He starts to say it again, *Mo-om*, but then sees that they're sitting too close for that.

The trip is eight songs long at truck-drying speed. 92.3, country, where the dials on all the tractors are set.

Jonas doesn't want to, but he knows every song, will forever.

They're not late, either, but already cars are having to park two and three blocks from the church. All the high school kids crying, their parents shepherding them, always keeping a hand to their backs.

Inside it smells like a church, like Bible pages and hymns, and Rob takes his hat off and they sit up in the family pews, Belinda having to carry Jonas' little brother when he can't walk in front of all these strangers.

All through the prayers and the song ("Amazing Grace") and the sniffling, Jonas reads the program he got at the door, imagines some conductor up front, nodding *now...now this, yes.*

It could be anybody.

But, no.

It could only be one person.

Larry Monahans, too tall for the front row, and never turning around to get a sense of the crowd, the congregation. Gwen beside him, not standing so well, then Sissy Holbrook, Earl edged in at the end of the pew, looking past the preacher, at the wall behind him maybe, the big wooden cross there.

If I had a snapshot of the four of them standing there, I wouldn't even need to be writing this, I don't think.

***

The cemetery's where it happens.

Dramatic, I know. But sometimes life really is, I guess.

For once, the wind isn't turned on, there's no grit in the air. Just blue sky for miles in every direction.

By the time Rob King cocks his truck up in the ditch across from the front gates, Stacy Monahans' casket is already graveside.

"Look there," Rob King says, leaning to the windshield for Belinda, "I'm not the only one, right?"

One of the guide wires for the utility pole, somebody's stretched it with a plow so that it's unraveling now, the pole starting to lean over, the way all the sagging cables are pulling it.

Belinda King shakes her head in exasperation—*this, now?*—but pats his cast on the seat all the same, and then they're serious again, all of them single-filing through the headstones, Rob leading, Belinda trailing, three kids between, holding hands like first grade. Like a family.

At least until Jonas says it, half under his breath but loud enough: "*Shit.*"

Belinda squeezes her hand around his some but Rob understands, looks up, ahead.

"Shit," he says as well.

The Midland County Sheriff is here. In uniform.

A few years down the road, Jonas will find a saddle for sale in the *Thrifty Nickel* for thirty-five dollars. It'll have California fenders on it, a chest harness, the works. For thirty-five dollars.

When he gets to the guy's house that afternoon, it's the Sheriff, retired, living alone, waiting it out.

He doesn't need the saddle anymore is the thing, is selling it cheap so long as whoever buys it promises to work it like it deserves, like it was made for.

Jonas will promise, sure, always keeping his hat brim down, his voice different, and fifteen years after that, he's still never put that saddle across a horse's back. Doesn't know where it might take him, what sunset he might have to ride into. Fall out the other side of.

"Rob?" Belinda King whispers forward, and Rob nods that he sees, yes, how could he not, and they keep walking.

Everybody from Greenwood is there too, even the basketball team, standing together, Geoff Koenig in a sling and sunglasses, always looking down, never up, where he might cross eyes with Larry Monahans.

Word later will be that they all showed up in their high-tops, but then Coach knew enough men in Lamesa that he was able to scrounge black dress shoes and boots for all of them. White socks against black leather, pleated pant legs never long enough, flapping.

If only that could be the main image of this funeral, I mean.

Pete Manson is there, though, leaning down for one last smoke at his truck before standing up for this with everyone else. Earl Holbrook up on the carpet grass with Sissy, his jaw muscle worrying, his left hand tight around hers. A hundred people Jonas doesn't know by name but recognizes all the same: him two years ago, when he was a shuffling kid, hands always nervous from wall ball; him in two years, always licking his lips, wanting nothing more than to explode out of this place; him in his twenties, dark from work, nervous that he's not out in the field right now, a wife beside him he can't even imagine but trusts will be there all the same, stepped up from the song she's been living in.

She is.

But this can't last forever.

Cue the woman Jonas never sees, on the other side of the crowd, just singing all at once the way happens at funerals, some song so beautiful and perfect it leaves his memory as he hears it. Stacy Monahans peaceful in her casket there, no brothers or sisters left behind. Just her. This distant shoot of the King family, snipped short.

Cue Pete Manson, grinding his cigarette out in the gravel then stepping forward, easing his hat off and trying— failing, like all the men—to smooth his thin hair down, look presentable.

Cue Rob King, after eye contact with Belinda—goodbye?— stepping forward through the mourners, to Earl, to be in the way should the Sheriff want to tap anybody on the shoulder of their nice jacket.

Cue Arthur King, parked close in his truck and sitting in it still, in his suit, Cecilia beside him, not to be trusted at solemn events these days but there as close as she can be anyway, her hat pinned to her hair, her hand to the dash like a child, to lean forward, see all this. People she remembers as other people, thirty years ago; forty.

Cue Tommy Moore, standing awkwardly from his mother's car, the first time he's been seen in weeks. It washes over the crowd, his presence. Like Hank Jr., he's in chrome sunglasses, a low-pulled hat, his face mostly hidden. Jonas looks up to Belinda so he can know how to react, and there's parentheses around her eyes, like she's hurting for Tommy Moore. It travels down her arm to her hand somehow, goes right to Jonas. Stays there.

Cue a row of birds diving in formation from the telephone wire when it shudders from some errant gust up there, the utility pole swaying with it. The birds fall into the breeze, spread their wings and turn as one, sweep low over the headstones.

Cue Jonas King, tracking the Sheriff.

Instead of taking his hat off like everybody else, he's making his casual way around the back of the crowd.

To Pete Manson's truck.

Not Earl's? Isn't that who he was asking after?

"Mom," Jonas whispers.

Belinda King looks up from the prayer—it was to be the year of prayers—sees the Sheriff too. And Pete Manson, looking right back at them.

She turns back to the burial. To the backs of everybody, her face set now.

"Mom," Jonas says again, pulling at her hand, a kid again, not really old enough to have been given a program like an adult.

Belinda King is watching her husband, though, and Rob King—he can see what's he done, now. To Tommy Moore.

But the Sheriff.

He's the one to pay attention to here.

Just doing his job.

Yeah.

Because Pete Manson's done with it, is leaving it behind, the Sheriff pinches his uniform pants up, squats down to retrieve the ground-out cigarette butt.

He holds it to his face, inspects it from one angle, from another.

It's probable cause. Close enough for West Texas.

He stands, stuffing the ashy butt into his shirt pocket, and reaches in through Pete's open window, for the crumpled cellophane pack on the dash, CHESTERFIELD there for the jury, so they won't have to look at blown-up photographs to know the brand, make the connection.

Except then that wall of birds, they swoop up, past. Not at the Sheriff or Pete Manson's truck, his flashy mirrors, just a random stupid thing—birds—but it's close enough.

The Sheriff flinches, drops the crumpled pack into Pete Manson's floorboard.

What he probably says here, during the prayer: "Shit."

Now it's not just Jonas King watching him.

For the first time, Larry Monahans' wide Stetson is turned to the side, a felt satellite dish.

Because he's the conductor here, everybody else turns to look as well, even the preacher, his Bible closed over his thumb now, to hold his place.

And Pete Manson?

He chuckles, shakes his head.

"Anything you need there, Jim?" he asks. The first name, not the office. Because this isn't Midland County, maybe. But still.

"Just this," the Sheriff has to say now, going ahead and just opening the door, pawing down in the floorboard for the Chesterfield pack.

Except.

This is where it happens.

Because it's bright outside, and he's got sunglasses on anyway, has to feel in the dark floorboard instead of really look, what the Sheriff's hand lucks onto isn't the pack, but a stock.

When he stands again, what he's got directed up into the sky—not at Geoff Koenig anymore is the push—is the most beautiful little .22 rifle. A Browning, the kind you load through the stock, so that whole balance of the gun is changed.

A murmur makes its way through the crowd, and Pete Manson has room now.

"Just shopping?" he says, "or you looking to make a purchase there?" The whole time just watching the Sheriff, not Larry Monahans, making his steady way through the mourners. The mourners parting before he's even there, like they've been rehearsing this all week, know their roles.

The only reason Pete Manson looks around, even, sees this coming, it's Gwen. What she says, already clamping her own hand over her mouth, it's "no."

It's too late, though.

Arthur King steps down from his truck, stands behind his door, the wind picking up now like it knows what's going down.

"We don't have to do this here," the Sheriff says then.

This is funny to Pete Manson. Like everything.

"Just a plinker," he says back, about the Browning. "Everybody here's got one, Sheriff."

By this time Larry's there, and the two of them: everything Pete Manson isn't, or ever will be, it's standing there over him now. Standing over him and accusing him of firing the shot that got his daughter to borrow that crap car, to try and drive later than she should have.

Pete smiles, taps his cigarette pack twice against his wrist and flicks his eyes straight to Belinda, Jonas thinks.

"This isn't about me, hoss," he says to Larry. "You know I don't mean to—"

He never gets to finish.

Larry's fist comes in high and fast from the outside, might as well be packed with dimes.

The only reason it doesn't connect: Rob King.

Larry's roundhouse pulls Rob into Larry—Rob rides it into him anyway—and Larry turns fast on him, has a look in his eyes Jonas King will see again years later, on Adam Moore, in a hundred parking lots.

Now the rest of the men are stepping forward, because Rob only has one arm, and this is Larry Monahans; there might not even *be* enough men here.

The Sheriff doesn't stop them, makes his way instead to Pete Manson. "For your own good," he says, turning Pete around for the cuffs.

Pete shakes his head in disbelief, looks to Belinda again, maybe, then to Larry Monahans and Rob King, then to the sea of black suits, all the serious faces.

"Check the trucks," he mumbles to the Sheriff, "everybody carries one, it's no damn crime, last I checked."

The Sheriff just ratchets the cuffs on, does a cursory pat-down, coming up with the pack of Chesterfields from Pete's shirt pocket, since the others are back in the truck.

"It's not the damn gun," he says, face-to-face with Pete now, "it's this."

What he means here is the pack of cigarettes, but what he and the rest of the funeral gets is something heavy and wrong and dark sliding down out of that cellophane sleeve, onto the grass.

The Sheriff and Pete and everybody look down, and then some Lamesa kid, maybe all of seven years old, probably grown up and selling life insurance now, or grinding the lenses of eyeglasses, he steps forward in his handed-down suit, picks up what dropped, passes it over.

What it is is a little lead slug, a magic bullet all deformed, stretched out like a finger.

Pete Manson thins his lips, shakes his head no.

"Pete Manson," the Sheriff starts, his tone slipping down into Miranda gear, but now Pete's dislodging him, shaking him off like nothing. Taking a full step away from the rights he's being read here.

"I didn't do it!" he says, no joke now, no smile, kind of blubbering, even.

Silence.

Nothing but.

Just the basketball team, stepping in front of Geoff Koenig, probably not even aware what they're doing.

"I didn't," Pete says again, looking around again at all the faces, his jury for today, and settling on one in particular, her eyes hot back at him, her hand too tight around her son's, and then she breathes in and steps forward, her voice not cracking at all, because she's been practicing as well: "He didn't," she says. "He was with me that morning."

Belinda King.

A whole different kind of silence now.

The Sheriff looks over at her.

"You sure, Lindy?" he says. "Haven't got your dates messed around there?"

Because it doesn't make sense, her giving alibi for Pete Manson, when Pete Manson can take her son's place on the gallows. To her son, it especially doesn't make sense. Shouldn't she *want* everybody looking to Pete for the fire? That way nobody's looking to Jonas for Geoff Koenig. It's stupid. He wants to tug her arm and tell her, to press her hand like during a prayer, to make eyes. To run away.

When he looks up to her, though, she pulls her hand away. She wants to be alone in this crowd.

Or she doesn't want to take anybody down with her.

Across from her, Pete Manson, smiling.

"What about this?" the Sheriff says, holding the slug up.

"A present for her," Pete says, nodding to Belinda, and now she closes her eyes, doesn't even open them when Rob King steps forward, finishes what Larry Monahans started, slamming his cast into Pete Manson's face.

Surgery three, yeah.

Because he's cuffed, Pete Manson can't stand up, just rolls on the ground and bellows, dirt all in his face, his hair.

Rob King steps forward to follow Pete down but now Larry Monahans is stopping him. Blood blooming on the white cast. Larry Monahans gives Rob King his hat, and Rob King sets it back on with his left hand, the dust rising from it as he does, his breath coming in heaves.

"You stupid shit," the Sheriff says to him then, to Rob King.

Rob King doesn't hear, is only looking to Belinda, who's not looking anywhere anymore, just down. Into her eyelids. Into a whole different decade.

Somebody helps Pete Manson up and he shrugs them off, says it so everybody knows what he's going to do here— "Robert!"—and charges headfirst forward for Rob King but there's too many people now, enough that they don't hear Jonas King at first. Just his voice, still high like a kid's.

What's he saying? Trying to say?

Again, the quiet.

Everybody looking down to him.

"Say again, son?" the Sheriff offers.

Jonas King looks side to side, blinks long, then opens his eyes, looks to his dad, and opens his mouth—

"I did it."

It doesn't come from Jonas King's mouth.

The crowd parts again.

At the end of that hall of bodies is Earl Holbrook, worrying his hat in his hands. He's staring at Jonas. "I did it," he says again, nodding over to Geoff Koenig.

"Bullshit." This from Larry Monahans.

Earl nods, won't look to Larry or his sister. Just Jonas.

"No," Jonas says, the shriek rising in his voice now, "no! It couldn't have—he's just—"

Earl shrugs it true, though.

Holds his wrists out, for the cuffs still on Pete.

Later, in court, his story will be that he didn't mean to, that he had been out in the field, was just holding the gun on that moving bus, saying what if, the crosshairs of his scope on no player in particular, no side glass at all, but then the gun went off somehow, just bucked in his hand. It wasn't a .22 at all either, like the first hole in the window suggested, but a .22-250, a centerfire round that's been around since 1937, was popularized just in time for World War II, and didn't need animation at all to punch through a bus.

As to why the jury will believe Earl Holbrook when he says all this: his two modules, his thirty or so bales there, they were the only ones uninsured.

He was gin manager, sure, but that was just until he could get it back together again farming-wise. Something he'd never be able to do now with this hit, this fire. And the land he was paying a quarter of his crop for? By rights, it should have been his wife's by inheritance, should have been his. He shouldn't have to be out scrapping, living on a shoestring.

It doesn't mean he pulled that trigger on purpose, though.

Just that he had reason to.

It'll be enough. Twice over.

"Earlybird?" Larry Monahans says across the crowd to Earl, and Earl just nods, once: yes, he killed Stacy Monahans. Your daughter, your only one. Yes, yes, yes.

Larry Monahans shakes his head no, no, it couldn't have been, it can't be, and the first step he takes forward like he has to, because he is who he is, Rob King's already there holding him back, but this time it takes all the suits, and more besides, until finally a shotgun blast silences them all.

Cue Arthur King at his truck, his stock set against his thigh, the barrel wisping smoke.

"Now then," he says, and somehow Stacy Monahans gets put in the ground that afternoon, and that's all it says in the *Lamesa Press-Reporter*: that services were held for the daughter of Larry and Gwen Monahans, and that she would be dearly missed.

They got the last part right, anyway.

Chapter Ten

The date, it's 1971.

The year Bowie's album *Hunky Dory* was released, probably never played in all of Midland or Martin Counties even once.

Buried on it, the 1973 hit "Life on Mars?"

A line from it: "to my mother, my dog, and clowns."

That was almost the epigraph for this, until I remembered Betty Underwood. I don't know if she'll remember saying what she said to me that day or not. If Ms. Godfrey will even tell her she's in this one.

So many things I don't know, really.

But some I do.

Or, I know who to ask, anyway, though I promised myself not to. That I was going to do this without her, not pull her back into it all again, just let it all be over, done with, gone.

I'm sorry.

1971.

There has to be an explanation for Belinda lying for Pete Manson at Stacy Monahan's funeral.

It has to have been a lie, I mean.

Never mind that for proof the next day, she offered the Sheriff a crumpled pack of Chesterfields from on top of the kitchen cabinet, where she was keeping them until Pete came around again so her boys wouldn't get into them. Rob sleeping at the hospital the night before and not home yet, maybe ever, provided his tractor never runs out of diesel.

1971, though.

Muhammad Ali goes down in Madison Square Garden, but gets back up. Jim Morrison goes down in Paris, doesn't get back up. Evil Knievel jumps nineteen cars at once. *All in the Family* starts its eight-year run. Vietnam, Intel, Walt Disney World. Duane Allman dies. JFK's still dead, Nixon in his place. Tornadoes, explosions, hostages. Somebody drives something on the moon.

None of that matters here.

All we'll need here, we've already seen it: kids, a truck, some beer, maybe a cigarette or two to make them feel grown up.

The truck's a Ford, probably, one surely parted-out by now but probably old even then, the kind nobody's going to care much if it's gone for the day, so long as it makes it back to the barn at some point.

And this is not at all where this was supposed to go, ever.

But she was always telling me, right?

This is the day Pete Manson's little brother goes under the truck.

Her hands when she tells me are nervous, her fingers always pinching at the air, like trying to find her next breath.

We're on the back porch of a different house, in a different part of Texas altogether, but, still, squint your eyes right and the CRP comes back, stands up through the concrete and the asphalt, and—there's no other way to say it—it beckons.

When I was twelve, and all the years around it, I could always take off through it when I needed to, just run until I fell down, the grasshoppers lifting up in a cloud of legs to take my place, keep moving the direction I was, rattle off into the distance for me.

It's what I want to do now, too.

So I can go back, whisper it to Jonas, make all the years between different? Tell Rob, get him to come in off the tractor finally?

I don't know.

***

As far as everybody was concerned in late January, the only reason Earl Holbrook was sticking to his story, that he was the one who shot Geoff Koenig, not Jonas, it was that if he ever stepped out from under the Sheriff's wing again, Larry Monahans, brother-in-law or not, would plant him where he stood. Simple as that.

In the *Midland Reporter-Telegram*, the trial coverage doesn't say anything about the fire, really, or about Stacy Monahans either. All that matters to them is what they call a "hunting accident involving a school bus," Earl Holbrook's .22-250 being of course a known varmint rifle, rabbits being no friend of any farmer.

It was the defense Earl Holbrook's public defender—Earl refused to bankrupt Sissy even more, just for him, though that in itself's a statement too, that she should have had land to sell, to buy him a proper defense—kept insisting upon, except, when Earl took the stand against all advice, he was quiet for a long time, getting his words together, the judge not even prompting him, and then he said it, what he'd been saying all along: that, yes, he was aiming at the bus; that, yes, his cotton had burned, with no recompense coming; that, yes, though he was at every game, still, at the time he did pretty much believe that those basketball players were the only ones who could have been responsible; that, no, he didn't remember pulling the trigger, not really. Just the rifle, bucking in his hands, but even that was slight, as heavy as the gun was, as light as the round was.

And, yes, he had helped the Sheriff's office search for the slug that day under something like false pretenses, but, no, there was no collusion of any kind with Pete Manson. Pete Manson wasn't holding that slug over his head, nothing as *Falcon Crest* as all that. Earl had just made a mistake, plain and simple. And then compounded it with more mistakes, each step no different than the last, until he was at the funeral that day in his best jacket, looking down on his only niece in a box.

Which is where he leaves it, more or less.

But that's hardly where it ends.

What he doesn't say is what he was doing that morning before the funeral: putting lock washers on either side of the two large u-bolts holding a backboard to a thick rusted pipe set in the ground some five or six feet. When the backboard, really, had hardly even been that loose.

But the pipe, the backboard.

The Sheriff's department was so blind.

The year before, playing hide-and-seek with his cousins at his grandparents', Jonas had, at the last possible moment before "100," decided his perfect place behind the riding mower wasn't so perfect after all and took off along the side of the house, rounded the corner just as the "ready or not" rang out behind him. Just as his cousin Audrey was clomping through the bushes, having heard Jonas running.

Out in the peach trees, Jonas could see his little brother trying to stand skinnier than he was behind a trunk, and, in the tall grass of a plow that was just getting shredded around now, another shirt.

And the footsteps are so close to him now, and Audrey, she's two years younger, sure, but she's faster than any of them, and there's nowhere to go. Back here it's just grass and the dogs' water bowl where they found the coachwhip last year and, and—

No time.

Desperate, giving up, Jonas looks straight up.

The roof's too high, of course—he's in fifth grade, still has to sneak up on top of the air conditioner first, which he's under strict orders never to do again—but projecting out from the roof like spokes, like the rays of light saints wear in paintings, are these handle-sized arms of wood. Probably stylish in 1960-whatever, and about to be again.

Jonas gathers himself, jumps higher than he ever has before, and hooks onto one of the low-hanging handles of wood with his right hand, manages to swing his left hand onto the next, and then pulls his body up flat under the eave, a reverse push-up, so that when Audrey comes around she just stands there not two feet under him, swiveling her head all around, finally seeing a knee behind a peach tree, taking off that way.

Behind her, in plain sight all along, Jonas unfolds himself down from the roof. He's a different person now. One who doesn't have to panic so much, but can take stock of his situation, come up with the only way out.

It's a completely different world.

Jonas smiles, walks over to base, is waiting there when Audrey comes back, so she has to do it all over again now.

"Where were you?" she says, out of breath.

For once, Jonas' little brother doesn't say anything, just smiles.

Jonas shrugs, nods his head for her to count again, and runs ahead a year so that he's sitting on a three-wheeler now. A little less than a half-mile in front of him, on Cloverdale, is a bus.

It's stopped, angled down into the ditch.

His mom is running towards it, her robe catching on the barbed wire fence. She turns around, rips it free so hard she goes to her hands in the ditch. But then she's there on the blacktop, didn't even look both ways twice, to be sure.

Jonas swallows, tries to see into the bus, and then a few minutes later the trucks and cars and sirens are all crowding around, a haze of dust hanging over them. There's men in the ditch, men in the road, men in their trucks, and finally Jonas pulls the clutch with his left hand, shifts down into first, is going to go help, at least see.

Except—the rifle. The .22.

There are police there, an ambulance now.

And something about the window midway down the side of the bus, everybody standing there, studying it, looking from there down some line of sight that ends in the open fields.

Jonas understands, feels it hollow in his chest.

What he's spent the morning doing is shooting at birds. With a rifle. Because it's what his mom's dad did with the cranes, an impossible thing. But the way his granddad had told it, what it was like to have them coating the sky black with their bodies, and then to aim up into that darkness, and pull the trigger, opening up a single column of light.

Jonas wants that. Wants to stand in that column of light for a moment.

Except the few birds he's been able to scare up, they're erratic, won't hold still for his sights.

How far can a .22 slug travel, though?

He has no idea. Couldn't even say for sure where he was each time he brought the stock to his shoulder.

They can't go as a high as a plane, anyway. He's tried, then closed his eyes, promised himself not to shoot at anything else all day, if those people up there can just get to their airport.

As high as a transformer, he guesses—okay, knows—up on the utility poles like a robot koala, like a dull grey porcupine. But he knows better than to shimmy up that creosote, feel the entry holes with his index finger, has seen the hawks and owls fried from that already.

This couldn't have been him, though, could it?

And, why him, with every kid with a rifle doing the exact same thing all across the county?

It's not fair.

He loves this gun.

But still.

Instead of winding up on the hand-grip, throttling a rooster tail of dirt up into the sky like usual, Jonas clicks up into second, burns the clutch a little trying to keep the pipe quiet, and turns around wide and dustless, his chest close to the gas tank, Indian style.

Where he goes is back to the basketball pad. Parks the three-wheeler as close to the tree as he can, so the seat won't heat up too much in the sun. Hooks the rifle over his shoulder and, making the ritual up as he goes, walks from corner to corner of the concrete pad, inscribing a deep, invisible X there.

On a map, it's where your treasure will be, yeah. Whenever you come back for it.

Finally Jonas shrugs, turns around to face the basket, hitches the rifle back to the center of his back and takes off running.

Just like with the wood arm reaching out from his grandparents' house a year ago, Jonas' fingers hang in the net just enough.

He swings his other hand around, his feet running in the air, finally finding the rusted pole.

After this, all he has to do is hand-over-hand it up the net—he's already up to the eighth hole on the pegboard in the old gym—grab onto the bird-shit back of the rim where the ball never can hit if it's aired up enough, and wrap his leg up onto the top of the pole. The top of the pipe.

With one arm hooked at the elbow in the rim, any kid not too worried about falling—worried more about jail—can let go enough with the other to shake a rifle sling down to his hand. Can hold on like that long enough to angle the barrel up into the uncapped top of that pipe, where his dad's been hiding his beer bottles, wedge it in at a painful, scratching-the-blueing-off angle, but then get it straight, let it drop down into that broken glass where nobody'll ever think to look. Not unless they're up there, say. Not unless they've stopped by because they promised to put a set of lock washers all around a couple of u-bolts. Not unless they're somebody who doesn't have any kids of their own to trade themselves in for.

And, the reason it's barrel-first is easy: Jonas doesn't want it filling with rainwater. Because he's coming back for it, isn't going to forget it.

That second part's true anyway.

***

This is what Larry Monahans will tell you in the drive-in in Lamesa one day over Chihuahuas, the Sky-Vue's specialty, the humped parking lot in front of the screen baking in the heat, the swings on the old playground up front sighing back and forth, you looking anywhere but at Larry:

- that he doesn't have to call you Doctor now, does he? Like Indiana? Good
- that he heard you could really shoot the ball before your ankle, yeah

- that—Robert ever tell you about that guy with the two teeth up in—?
- that yeah, he's the same age as Robert, give or take some months. That he never called him Uncle
- that—it's just beans, mostly. Nothing to worry about— or, something for everybody else to worry about, right?
- that yeah, if it's so important, his dad did sire him at sixteen, just taking his dad's lead, who'd had Sterling at seventeen, young enough to scare his ass off diapers for, what, fifteen years? Robert and Parker and the little one, Jackson? Sixteen years? Shit, man
- that—was Arthur King a Civil War buff or what?
- that he never thought about that before
- that you did your homework, sounds like. He was fifteen when Stace was born, sure. Family tradition. A freshman. But her mom was a junior then already, and a varsity cheerleader at that
- that—put that in your book, yeah
- that—are you going to finish that or just push it the fuck around?
- that he hadn't heard Pete was working the tables nowadays. But it makes sense. Every season's a crapshoot
- that no, he never knew any of the Ledbetter girls
- that no, he didn't know Rooster either. He a cartoon or something?
- that, okay: a dead cartoon?
- that the funnel cakes are good if you eat them fast enough, yeah
- that "Macinaw" is how it is on the birth certificate, as far as he knows. That you can check yourself. Just put it on your little list there

- that, last he heard, Sissy was off in Dallas somewhere. That maybe she'll be in one of your classes one day, wouldn't that be a hoot?
- that that field's never done lower than two bales an acre since then, no
- that—your mother, she had you when she was what? Fifteen?
- that she was a cheerleader too, no offense
- that you wouldn't even be here if he hadn't made some certain introductions, did you know that?
- that—was there any famous Larry in the Civil War?
- that he just thought you might know, being a doctor and all
- that, speaking of, he's got a pain right—oh, right across the table here, looking back at him, writing everything down like it matters
- that he heard you can only hunt in certain sections up there, like a lottery or something
- that when he was seventeen, he drove through that fence by the drive-in screen, on that side, going about sixty
- that they had to stop the projector and everything
- that it was that Billy the Kid movie. Right at the end of summer, almost
- that—Dylan who?
- that he's got other rats to kill today, yeah
- that no, it's on him
- that he doesn't know what the song was, sorry
- that he hardly ever thinks about all that anymore
- that—was there something else you wanted to ask here?
- that he didn't think so
- that you should tell your mom hey

- that—could you maybe write him a doctor's note, so he could go home, read books all day or something?
- that it's on him, really.

What Larry Monahans won't tell you, even though both of you pretty much know this is the last time either of you will ever sit across a table from each other:

- that Stacy was five before he really became her father
- that he spent the next ten years trying to make up for that
- that she was named after his dad, kind of
- that she never knew that.

What you say to yourself, sitting at that table after he leaves, racking his pipes up on 349, announcing to all of Lamesa that he's still here, that he's not going anywhere:

- that you're going to have to use a list or something for him
- that you don't trust yourself with a scene
- that he doesn't deserve it
- that you don't owe him anything
- that, "bullet points"—is that a joke?
- that you'll call him Larry anyway
- that he'll never read it
- that—"sire?"
- that it was probably a Ford Sterling did it in
- that you know it wasn't
- that you can make it be a Ford anyway
- that you're not doing that this time
- that it would be perfect, though

- that nobody would know
- that nobody would say anything anyway
- that Parker isn't a Civil War name
- that Dylan isn't either
- that Geoff might be
- that your ankle's fine, thank you
- that that doesn't mean that tooth story's real
- that you could read aloud better than anybody in your graduating class—the class you should have graduated with
- that his yearbook photo, when you turn one page back—it was all right there
- that nobody saw it
- that you'll write him a note, sure. One about three hundred pages long, say?
- that—does he know he was almost a clown?
- that—"bullet points." It's not a joke at all
- that Gwen's still waiting.

***

Walking back through Arthur King's abandoned trucks and tractors one day before all this—1983, say—Rob King points to a truck for Jonas, says to count the faded cans on the dash, there through the windshield.

Jonas does: nineteen.

Rob King nods, doesn't stop walking.

"Why?" Jonas finally says, stepping over the tongue of a long-dead trailer.

Rob King shrugs, says, "I don't want you drinking, you know?"

Jonas keeps walking too.

"They're yours, aren't they?" he says.

"Forget it," Rob King says, and for a while Jonas does.

But then he gets a .22 a year or two later, and a .22's not even a gun with no cans to plink, right?

When the doors of the old truck—a Chevy stepside, 1967—are jammed shut, either locked or rusted, it doesn't matter: the back window's gone, cleaned out.

Jonas climbs in, takes the cans out four at a time.

He doesn't know the whole story yet, though.

And, if he doesn't take those cans, he never will.

***

Non-fiction, man.

Right now, and forever, Jonas is behind Arthur King's house, smuggling the past into his present like only a twelve-year-old can, and there's something else I know happened too, right around then. Something that had to have happened for any of this to make sense, except I don't know the when of it, exactly.

In a real live novel, in fiction, it would be at the exact same time, wouldn't it?

Jonas would be planting one hand on the side of that 67 Chevy's bed, vaulting down, trying not to let all those cans rattle, his mouth set in a thin, determined line, while just fifty yards directly to the south, in Arthur King's house, his wife Cecilia would be laying into him with her fists and arms, her feet and teeth, whatever she could reach, swing, throw.

This is sixteen years after the last time she went after him. When Sterling died.

It's easy to let all the years and people mix together, I know.

Mouse died in World War II, a hero.

Sterling shot himself the year Hot Wheels hit the shelves.

His granddaughter Stacy would hit her sheet of water in 1986, ride it like glass for maybe the length of a football field, roll to a stop in the turnrow of a cotton field, her hands still on the steering wheel, the car off, dead, the sun coming up for her through what had been a windshield, was just air now, nothing between her and the morning anymore. Or ever again.

And, in this summer of 1984 I'm reaching back for, Belinda King is in the big house, her in-laws' house. Not to visit, but because Rob's asked her to check on his mom.

You dress it up as coffee, though, of course.

What you're doing is keeping an old woman from doddering off into her head, never coming back.

And what Belinda King's thinking, sitting across the table from Cecilia King, is that it's too late.

I think this did all happen at the same time, the same day, that one morning. It had to have.

Sometimes life, it is a story.

"Rob doesn't even have any pictures of him," Belinda is saying, just casual, another thing to talk about since they're just sitting there.

Cecilia looks up her about this and there are cards shuffling in her head, photo albums spilled all over the floor, the dust still rising from them.

But she comes up with the right snapshot, the right name: "I named him that to protect him, did you know that?"

"Sterling," Belinda says, trying to track this.

"Your silver," Cecilia says, reaching across to pat the top of Belinda's hand like a woman should know this, "you only take it out for special occasions. And then you put it back where it goes."

Belinda nods like this makes perfect sense, sips some heat from her cup and becomes aware of her father-in-law standing in the doorway in his boots, like he's just going out to the shop, or the field. To do something with his day, something small and unimportant.

But this little scene had stopped him.

He's just standing there, studying his wife.

Slowly, she looks up to him.

"Cecilia," Arthur King says, and it sounds for all the world to Belinda like a warning.

Cecilia doesn't look away from him for even an instant.

"It was supposed to keep him safe," she repeats, right to Arthur King, and he shapes his mouth around some word, some series of words to pat her down, but it's too late.

Cecilia King comes across the table at him, finds him, driving both of them back into the wall so that Belinda is sitting there at an overturned kitchen table, her coffee saved at the last instant.

She breathes in, out, then sets her coffee on the counter behind her, lifts Cecilia King's ninety pounds from Arthur King, who isn't even fighting back.

The two of them—Cecilia, Lindy—fall back into the kitchen, Belinda turning to take the brunt of the impact, keep Cecilia from cracking a hip.

And still she has to hold her until the thrashing is done, shifts down to crying. To giving up. Again.

Before she leaves, Belinda rights the table. Closes the front door Arthur King left open behind him. Settles Cecilia into her bed.

"I'm sorry," she says, because there's nothing else.

She crosses back to her and Rob's little house, and his truck's pulled up to it, the door open, meaning he just forgot something, isn't there for long.

She quickens her pace, catches him in the kitchen, his thermos in his hand.

"Tell me about Sterling," she tells him.

Rob King stops by the dryer, sets his thermos deliberately down on it. His eyes looking hard through the rusted screen door. Where he almost was.

"He just, you know," he says.

Belinda turns him around, holds him by the arms.

"He killed himself," she says. "But why?"

"Lin—some people just—"

"He's your brother, goddammit," she says. "You know."

"Why?"

"Because I'm part of this now. I'm a King, aren't I? Aren't our kids Kings? Isn't this a King house? King land?"

Rob laughs a nervous laugh, his lips exactly like Cecilia's in her weaker, most lost moments.

He covers it with his hand, flashes his eyes at Belinda then turns away. Is reaching for his thermos already.

"It was your dad," Belinda says then, behind him.

Rob stops again, his back to her.

He swallows, presses his eyes closed.

Belinda lays her face alongside his back, is blinking fast to have to know this.

"It wasn't his fault," Rob says, his voice miles away. "His dad, my granddad, he, he—"

"And Sterling was his—he was the one he, he . . .?" Belinda says, bringing her hands up to her husband's shoulders.

"Sterling told him if he ever touched us, he'd burn the whole place down," Rob says, his voice breaking so that Belinda knows better than to turn him around, make him face her. "He—he traded himself for us, Lin, he thought he could carry it all, could forget it, that it would stop with—"

"I can't stay here," Belinda says, closing her eyes against the smoky fabric of Rob King's jacket. "I don't care where we go this time, but I can't, Rob."

They stand there. They breathe.

"I'll build a house," Rob King says at last. "It'll be perfect, it won't be like this at all. And he'll never—"

But now Belinda's pushing away from him. Turning her head like to look through the walls of the little house. Out to all the derelict equipment. All the history rusting into the weeds. To the horses, watching her back.

"Jonas," she says. "Rob, your—Arthur. He left the house a few minutes ago, he, he," and she's already at the door now, slamming it open, letting the wind slap it against the side of the house, stepping out onto the concrete block of a porch.

"*Jonas Allen King!*" she screams, loud enough that she has to lean forward to do it, "Jonas Allen King, if you can hear my voice—"

He still can.

***

A field, some beer, a truckful of kids on a Saturday afternoon.

This isn't a book about Hot Wheels anymore, isn't a book about phones.

This is about those kids.

Pete Manson's little brother was Tray.

It starts in Lamesa, though.

Larry Monahans, nearly sixteen, able to pass for eighteen, crunches the emergency brake down on his dad's old green Ford and leans forward, shuts his eyes against the cloud of dust he's been pulling for the last few miles.

After it passes, Kenneth Brown is standing there against the cattle guard, his little sister Belinda with him. She's squinting.

"What about Earlybird?" Larry calls out through the window.

"I look like his mother?" Kenneth says back, bringing his shoulders up, offended but not really.

"Like somebody's," Larry says back, nodding down to Belinda.

She's fourteen here.

Like with Tray, later, what Belinda is for Larry and Kenneth is assurance that they won't be drinking and carrying on.

Not two miles out of town, she looks to either side of her, Larry and Kenneth, and threads a cigarette up from her handed-down purse, punches Larry's lighter in, just looks straight ahead until it pops back out.

"Mind?" she says, applying the cigarette to her lips like lipstick, so adult.

Larry smiles and shakes his head in wonder, drapes his arm behind her to kick the split rear window open.

Kenneth doesn't say anything, is letting her smoke all she wants—more, even; this way, there's no chance of her saying anything about the beer Larry's already slowing down for, his pipes popping, his jaw set like a twenty-year-old.

Another Saturday in West Texas.

Two blinks, the sound of cans ripping open, and they're in Stanton, ducking under the interstate, meeting up with Pete Manson.

They almost make it away from his place, too, but then Mrs. Manson meets them at the cattle guard so that they're all gripping their beer cans between their boots now, the emergency brake on the old Ford ratcheted all the way down again.

"There even enough seatbelts?" Mrs. Manson says, leaning up from her station wagon.

On the bench seat, they're three across, Belinda a feather on Pete Manson's lap, his hand on the side of her thigh to keep her from sliding off.

When Mrs. Manson had crested the cattle-guard four seconds ago, her chrome bumper blinding them all for a flash, Belinda had taken his beer as calmly as if it were the offering plate at church, done something floorboard-ish with it.

Is he in love here, a little?

Who wouldn't be.

In the months to come, the years, he'll look back to her taking his beer with her perfect hands that day as a sign that this was their first date. That this is how things happen. How they should have happened. To prove it to her, he'll even filch a twisted piece of lead up from the shoulder of a fast road one day, a piece of lead that could be the balance weight for a tire, could be a flattened battery terminal connector, could be a hundred things, but isn't.

What it is, for him, is a clutch of roses, fifteen years too late.

Her son, delivered back to her. By him. To show her.

Except.

Except that piece of lead, that slug, it finally won't be from a rimfire gun. Will be much higher velocity. The kind juries can hear. The kind they have to hear. The kind that makes everything true, never mind the blonde woman screaming in the courtroom, reaching out to touch her husband's hand again, like they used to at basketball games, on weeknights.

But that's all later, doesn't matter here.

What matters here is a twelve-year-old in the backseat of a station wagon, asking if he can go with, Mom? Please?

Mrs. Manson turns her severe, insurance-receptionist face to the truck rumbling beside her, says, "You're not going anywhere Tray can't go, are you?"

The only answer here is no. Of course not.

Moms have been playing this game forever.

So, shuffle one kid out a back door, and then, because the station wagon's still there waiting, let him in front, strap him into the place his big brother just volunteered.

In the bed of that truck, now, it's Pete Manson, holding onto the bed rail, and Belinda Brown, half under his arm, falling into him again and again.

"Where are we going?" she says up to him, her voice shaking from the wind.

They're on 137, blasting south across the tracks.

"Greenwood, probably," Pete says, leaning out the side to eyeball the right turn to Cloverdale. "Larry's got an uncle there."

"An uncle?"

Pete shakes his head no, it's nothing to worry about, and holds his can out to her. She takes it, looks around as if to be sure, and takes a sip, laughs about it.

What Pete says, taking the can back, it's "canteen kiss."

Belinda doesn't say it isn't.

***

Not ten minutes later, the glasspacks on the green Ford are popping. They're slowing down to make the turn into the King place.

It's where they find Rob. Pete never had a chance.

Rob King is about halfway between the front house and the new barn. Not sitting in the broke-down truck but lying longways in it, his boots James Deaned out the passenger window, his head against the driver's armrest, a line of cans on the dash, one of his hands up in front of him like he's got a toy, is playing with it, swooping it under clouds, over buildings.

Finally Larry has to race the engine of the Ford up, shatter the moment Rob was just pretending was there in the first place.

"What?" he creaks out, then hooks an elbow up onto the lower lip of the missing back window, wrenches himself up, the day too bright for him.

"Go away," he says, just generally. "I'm thinking."

In response, Larry and Kenneth and Pete pelt the cab of the truck he's in with cans, so that he has to turn a shoulder, roll away. Clambering out the driver's door he stuffs his hand deep into his pocket, like hiding something, but comes up with a set of keys, locks the door behind him.

"Stupid shit," Larry says, because the truck has no back window.

It's the same way you lock your tree house, though, even when there's no roof.

"Uncle stupid shit to you," Rob says, and Larry steps forward, ready for their fight, and they punch chests and shoulders, tackle each other into the dry weeds, come up with seedheads golden in the air all around them, and this is when Rob King first lays eyes on Belinda Brown, in the back of that truck.

Like I said: Pete never had a chance.

***

Two hours later, Tray Manson is dead.

And if there were a way I could just leave it like that, I would.

It pays him no respect for me to place his head under that tire again. To say something about pumpkins, just to establish it's Halloween.

I wasn't there, I mean.

He died before I was ever born.

I've been to his headstone in Stanton, sure, my grand tour of West Texas cemeteries, "research," but it's just a piece of polished rock, some words. The grass around it not even manicured like it is around Stacy Monahans' grave in Lamesa.

What I tell him, standing there, is that it's not his fault.

And that I'm going to have to write about it. That that's the only way.

What I don't tell him is that his big brother hasn't returned from his last trip to Vegas yet. That maybe that means he's having a good run, that he's been awake for five days now, taking cards, pushing chips.

What I don't tell him is the picture I have of Pete Manson in my head. This big guy in a cap and overalls, walking by himself under all that neon, waiting for the house to let him win at last, because he deserves it. Because he never told anybody.

But already he's mixing in my head with Buford Wilson from the Tanya Tucker song. Buford Wilson who carried a letter in his overalls for years, Buford Wilson, who nobody would talk to, Buford Wilson who finally died in the street, none of his questions ever answered.

Pete Manson, I'm sorry.

And thank you.

This is for you.

1971.

You're in the back of a green Ford, bouncing through a field to an old falling-down house that King guy knows, and it's a near-perfect day. A pretty girl beside you, half under your arm sometimes, a girl who isn't from Stanton so doesn't remember what you did in the fourth grade that time, a girl you're only just now, from the way Larry introduced her, realizing is Kenneth Brown's grown-up little sister.

But Kenneth doesn't care.

In the cab, all he's doing is ribbing Larry about his sister and Earlybird's worm, Larry gunning the truck then stomping on the brakes again each time Kenneth tries to drink, everybody in the bed trying to roll with it.

As for the falling-down house they're going to, the King guy says it's been empty forever already. That his big brother used to take him there, show him all the old stuff, like walking through a museum. And this brother used to scare him with that house too, about how the Reverends Green and Wood used to live there, that it was a church then, the first one in these parts, except, digging the cellar, they cut the arm off somebody already buried, so that now that dead guy walks the rooms, always just behind you, reaching out to you with his left arm, trying to see if you're the one who has his other one, his good one. Or if he can borrow yours, maybe.

When the King guy had told that, Tray had gone pale but tried to smile it off, and Belinda had just shook her head, not believed it.

Get her in that old house, though, and it might be a different story. She might want to press up against somebody, to be safe.

It's an old game too.

Except.

One of the times Larry guns it, splashing Kenneth's chin with beer at last, Tray topples out the back, over the tailgate. Just as quiet as can be.

"Hold!" the King guy calls ahead, and Larry steps on the emergency brake again, the only real brake this truck has.

"Lose one?" Larry says into his mirror, ducking the beer Kenneth's trying to tip onto him, his smile sharp in the rearview but then gone again.

"Just let him—" you start, not eager to remove yourself from this girl, but now the King guy's got his hand up anyway, is guiding the truck back but is mostly just watching Kenneth shake a beer up, his fingers to the tab already, the afternoon ready to explode.

And then the girl who was so close to you, she's at the tailgate, leaning over, saying it once, loud, using the name Larry used to introduce him—*Robert!*—and you lean over too, to see what's the matter here, and the emergency brake crunching down pushes you even farther out, so you have to see, and—and afterwards, after this afternoon explodes, after everybody knows it was stupid, that it was nobody's fault, that if it was anybody's, it was Larry Monahans', who never says word one about it, just that yes, it was him at the wheel, after all of this, the girl, instead of consoling you about your brother, she finds the King guy.

He's back in that broke-down truck he sits in again, is hitting himself in the sides of the head because it's his fault, because it should have been his head under that tire, and, because she was there, because she knows it was all of their faults, really, not just Larry's like everybody's saying, she opens that door, leads him away from that truck, into the rest of his life, a life that should have been yours. A life you can only watch now.

What you would have said earlier, in response to the question I didn't ask, about what you did after that day: You're still doing it.

I understand.

III

Chapter Eleven

What else.

I know. Ten chapters is such a good, even number. As far as I meant to go.

But, eleven, those two parallel lines trying to touch—book eleven is where Odysseus performs the sacrifices that bring up the souls of the dead, right?

Jonas is that sacrifice, I think.

After telling her story, using her hands to both show and hide Tray Manson's head under the tire that day, Belinda King stands up, walks out to the edge of her new porch, where the flagstone shelves out over the grass.

It's July, late.

"Now you know," she says, laughing a little about it but not really. Using the side of her index finger to guide something out of her eye.

Now you know.

Of the dead, the people in the ground, there's Mouse, there's Sterling, there's Stacy Monahans, there's Tray Manson, and there's even Rooster Jones, his plastic ear probably the only thing left of him down there anymore.

And there's one more.

By the middle of March, 1986, Earl Holbrook has been convicted and sentenced.

This is the exact middle of the economic sag between the early eighties and the late eighties, though; the county holding facilities are packed, not just with people trying to drink until the next boom, make the last one last anyway, but with people with their faces painted green, sleeping it off.

In the courtroom that day, all the Greenwood farmers are there. Not because they don't think Earl Holbrook's guilty—the ballistics proved it was him, made the case for the district attorney, and Earl had confessed anyway—but because he's one of them. It's weak to say, maybe, but it's real, too. My single most distinct memory of the sixth grade, it's the week I had to sit at the lice-head table, all by myself some days, and how my friends, and I can't even remember what names I'm using for them now, don't want to look—Brett and Steve and Teddy and Robert and Asael and Clayton and Lloyd and Randy, okay?—how they all filed out of the serving line but then swung wide, closer to my table than anybody else would, and held their hands out as they passed, to slap five with mine. This is what those other farmers were for Earl Holbrook the day he was sentenced, the day his five years of state time was supposed to start.

There but for the grace of God, all that.

It was a school day for all of us, though.

Basketball, to be specific.

Because varsity always got the big gym, we had to use the practice one, with the rubber floor that would throw you into the wall if it wasn't squeaky clean.

Between the two was a hall, the one Jonas had used to sneak out of the tournament a couple of months ago. Or, the hall he'd used to sneak back in, so he could make his big escape.

It doesn't matter.

Earl Holbrook was sentenced by ten in the morning, and then it was just all the farmers milling around in front of the courthouse, waiting for Earl to be led out to the blue bus.

Pete Manson is there, grinding a cigarette out then collecting it, putting it in his pocket. Rob King, in a new cast. Arthur King, still years from his own grave, wearing the same suit he'd worn to Stacy Monahan's funeral.

Ten minutes before noon, the deputies or marshals or bailiffs or whoever does this finally lead Earl and three other prisoners up the ramp from the basement. He's still in his trial suit. No orange jumpsuit yet. And he manages to smile, even, at everybody there, nodding goodbye. All of them making promises to themselves that, when he comes back, if they ever have any extra work, it's his.

No Sissy, of course, but that's just because she got to say bye inside. She isn't going to Lamesa to live with her parents or her brother—never that—but'll find something to do until Earl's out again.

About this time, Coach Harrison is rolling the television set out into the hall between the two gyms. It's on a two-level plastic tray that was once intended for towels, probably.

It's on, too, this television. The news.

We dribble for a while, don't have any drills to do, and one by one cue into Coach, start to look into that hall.

He's not watching the noon update about Earl Holbrook's case.

1986 is the year Halley's Comet passes, but it's not that either.

In Midland, the prisoners seated now, staggered out two on one side, one alone on the other—Earl—the bus folds its doors into itself, grinds away.

For a few minutes, until everybody can decide where to eat, maybe—Monterey's, on the east side—there's just milling, shuffling. Pete Manson flaring another cigarette up against the day, blinking through the smoke at Rob King, talking to Jenkins now, making some joke or another about his new cast, Jenkins looking away, smiling his cop smile. Arthur King having serious words with the Sheriff, it seems, probably apologizing for all of this. Trying to mend what fences can still be mended. The Sheriff tilting his hat back on his head and watching the bus turn north, nodding to Arthur King. Nodding again, sure, then looking at his watch, remembering some other place to be.

This is how stories end, with all these leftover characters, nothing left for them to do.

These are real people, though.

In the hall between the two gyms, Coach Harrison waves us in, tells us we need to see this, and we edge in, crowd the screen, don't know what to say.

Forty miles north, give or take—forty-two and six-tenths, exactly, thirty-eight and a smidge if you take 137—Earl Holbrook is sitting in his seat. What he's doing is watching the cotton slip past. Looking down every row he can, like, if he can just focus on one for long enough, he'll see straight down it maybe, right to the center of everything. See why that trigger had to be so touchy that day, the air so still for the first time ever, maybe. See why Geoff Koenig had to choose that moment to be walking through that part of the bus.

But they're both on buses now.

It's fitting, he thinks, and has the leading edges of a smile starting around his mouth when he cues into a tractor just ahead, waiting for the bus to pass so it can turn around, swing its plow into the road, not take any guide wires with it.

Except.

Except the plow hitched onto that tractor, it's not stalkcutters, it's not discs, it's not a breaking plow, it's a knifing rig.

Why would anybody be tied onto a knifing rig when the seed's not even in the ground yet?

And then Earl sees the man up in that cab, that pulled-down way he wears his hat, how he tucks his long sleeves into his gloves, and it's his best friend from high school. His best friend, who told Earl he wouldn't trust his sister with anybody else, serious.

Larry Monahans times it perfect, from years in that seat. He throttles ahead a jump, mashing the left brake sharp so the tractor pirouettes around in the ditch, the leading right edge of the knifing rig slicing up over the road, into the side of the bus Earlybird's on, each knife three feet long, polished by miles of sand, and Earl Holbrook only has time to hold his hands up before his face—they're chained to the floor—only has time to close his eyes, to tell Larry that he understands, that if he'd only ever had a child, it might be him up there in that yellow seat, out there, if only—

And then it's over.

On the news that night, the whole episode gets maybe a minute and a half.

It's an accident between a tractor and a prison bus, not even in Midland County. The only newsworthy bit about it, even, it's that the farmer driving that tractor—nothing about a knifing rig, nothing about that being the low place on 349 where a girl died back in January, the first fatality of the new year for Dawson county—the only thing, according to the scraped-up bus driver, is that that farmer, he came down from his tractor and stepped onto that bus with a lever-action .44-40, and kept the two remaining prisoners in their seats until the authorities showed up, and how you could tell he was regretful, it was because he was crying, looking down the barrel of that rifle.

It was an accident.

And the reason it only gets ninety seconds: In the hall between the gyms that day, what we're all watching, some of us crying, because some secret part of us is still sure we can be astronauts too, is Challenger, spread out across the sky, falling, falling, Michael Graham maybe going home that day after school and finding his old list from fourth grade, adding this to his list of things that have been taken away, and then letting that list go as well, across the field, a prayer of sorts, for all of us.

/

∗∗∗

The day after Earl Holbrook's funeral, Jonas King wears one of Earl's old hats to school. It's the Stetson, is too big, is black and furry even, ridiculous, and Jonas has his mule-eared boots on too, and even his friend who said Ms. Everett's name that time, he just nods to Jonas, standing alone at his locker long after class has started, then stands there a couple of lockers down until Jonas is ready, so it's two people being late instead of just one.

And I want this to just be through already.

But there's still the sacrifice.

Not the Jonas who finds his uncle's shiny chrome rig in the church parking lot after school that day, goes to eat with him for the whole afternoon, and not the Rob King who was this same age once too, standing behind the house in his t-shirt and underwear one early morning, watching his dad use three hoses at once to wash a big brother's brains out the back of a truck, but maybe the Jonas from before all this started, the Jonas trying to carry four old beer cans at once but dropping one into the floorboard, going after it, coming up instead with

an old cardboard backing, the slick kind with a tab to hang by. It's been lodged under the seat for years, so the sun hasn't faded the words from it yet. The model.
But no. Not yet.
I've still left one scene open.
Two, really.

***

"Let's pray for your father," Belinda King says to her sons the day the trampoline blows away, the day the pump house explodes, and they do, holding hands behind the sliding glass door, the air still full of trash outside, grit in all the sills, fine like from an hourglass.

This is the week before the fire. Maybe ten days.

Just after Thanksgiving, always a bad time for her, now that she knows about Arthur King. The one time of the year she has to put on a good face, has to see him sitting there so content with himself, like he's getting away with everything.

But she watches her boys when they're over there, she watches them close even though he's old now, has to be retired from all that. He'll have have to answer for what he's done, sure, but not to her, right?

It's the peace she's come to over the last few months

Otherwise Rob'll have no land to farm. Otherwise they won't be able to keep paying for this house.

"Dear Lord," she leads off, all of their eyes closed, and tries to will her husband safe, home again, and then leaves the boys with some cartoons, goes outside to try to get ahead of this trash eddying all around, rising just to fall again, and the prayer, it works. Rob King makes it home again that night, like always, like all the farmers always do, never mind the lightning, the wind, the machinery, the hundred ways to die out there.

Being a farmer's wife, you have to trust that your man's capable, and, after that, just leave it up to God's will, right?

Right.

But when she comes in from cleaning up the trash, her hands black from the burn barrels—Jonas doesn't know.

"Mom?"

She pulls her mouth into a smile, shakes her head no, nothing—"just thinking about your father, dear"—and she sleepwalks through the next week and a half, until, one morning, the boys' pants in the dryer again for school, she looks over to Rob with his coffee at the kitchen window, sees how far outside he's looking. How intentionally.

"Do you have to set them up like that?" he says, low enough that the boys won't hear.

Like—?

She turns to the table: three boys eating cereal in their underwear, waiting for their pants to get warm.

"What if—what if somebody comes to the door?" he says, still looking through his own reflection, to the fields outside.

"They're just boys," Belinda says, smiling, her coffee to her mouth again, and then hears herself, hears her husband, and dabs her lips, manages to turn slightly away without dropping her cup.

But her hand's shaking around it.

All day.

And her son, her oldest, this Jonas, if he stands up right that moment, if he walks a straight line from their front door, steps out across the CRP, across the pasture, clipping the corner of Rooster's big field, where he'd be a quarter of a century later is in the cemetery behind the Greenwood church. The one he chased balls into at recess. It's the place he's been avoiding now for ten chapters. The place he's waiting for, so he can say he did it the best he could. That it's on paper now.

But then it's not all on paper. Not yet.

There on Earl Holbrook's weathered headstone, it's a little car, a Hot Wheels, and, and.

Reach for it.

Don't touch it.

Remember it.

Try not to.

Evil Weevil.

How Jonas knows the model is that when he was twelve, digging for cans in an old truck behind his granddad's house, he found the slick cardboard backing for this car, wedged up under the seat like a joke—in Greenwood, Texas, all weevils are evil—and put it in his pocket to show his dad, ask him about it, but then used it for target practice instead, after all the cans were gone, and that was that.

Except.

Except Rob King wasn't the one to put that little car at Earl Holbrook's grave either, as apology, his most sacred thing, the thing he found under the seat one October day like his big brother had left it just for the twelve-year-old he'd been, the toy he opened then hid in his pocket the afternoon he met his wife.

No.

And this is the part where Jonas dies, goes away forever.

The day after the trampoline blew away, what he found in the CRP behind the house, it doesn't make sense until he sees that little car at the base of that headstone.

What he found back in the grass, just moving from yellow blade to yellow blade, like he was supposed to follow it, had to for maybe half an acre, was a single magazine page. Half a page, really.

But that page.

It's a boy's leg, no pants on, no underwear.

For years after he burns it in the barrels, getting in trouble for playing with matches but who cares, he'll think it just blew in from some other place, like all the cusswords his mind spit back exactly when the Sunday school teacher told him they were sins.

The little car, though.

Yes, he's seen it before.

It was in the back corner of his dad's top drawer, rubber-banded to a yolky old photograph.

But his dad never came back for it, for any of his stuff, he left Belinda to clean it out, store it in the garage, finally throw it out, even though her sons had been pinching shirts from it for years already.

What he never understood, Rob, could never explain away, were those cigarettes up on top of the kitchen cabinets. The ones with a tax-stamp date the Sheriff's office never thought to check, the same way they never thought to ask themselves why Arthur King had taken such a casual interest in what route Earl Holbrook's prison bus was going to take up to Lamesa, say. The same way they ruled an accident what makes perfect sense when you take into account that Arthur King had one of those truck phones, and Larry Monahans did too, and that they were both Kings, and that, years and important years ago, Larry Monahans had taken some bad heat for Arthur King's son, heat for backing over a twelve-year-old, heat that could have sent Arthur King's last best chance of a son spinning out into a completely different life, what with his brother already a suicide and all.

But Rob's there anyway.

Where he is now, it's an old house, a tore-down and buried house, a house plowed under now, along with the concrete pad laid down beside it, and that concrete pad's basketball pole, and whatever was in that pole. He's in an old house that's been there forever, and his right arm was never quite fixed, never got straightened out again, so what he does now is walk from room to room, tugging at your sleeve, seeing if you've got his good arm, if you can explain all of this to him maybe.

And you can explain it.

You don't want to, but you can. For him.

The day after the trampoline blew away, this mom, this farmer's wife, see, she walks out into the backyard to try to get ahead of the trash all blowing around, and then, like a message, it just settles all around her, and it's the other half of the page her son will find the next day. It's all the other halves of all the pages, it's why her husband's always said there's only one key to the pump house.

And it's not his fault either.

It's his father's fault.

His goddamn father. That monster. All his cotton out there waiting to get turned into more money, more reward.

Yeah.

This is what Pete Manson never tells anybody, this is the reason Belinda King lies for him at Stacy Monahans' funeral: there's these kids in a truck, on a Saturday, and they're drinking and it's not too hot and not too cold, and at some perfect moment in that day, this beautiful girl from another town, she reaches her hand down across the tailgate, passing her already-lit Chesterfield to an awkward boy who'll smoke that brand from here on out now, in honor. Who will recognize that brand by all the black modules, and will fold that information into his overalls and keep it there forever, until he finally loses himself in a city he doesn't know, maybe following a twelve-year-old boy he thinks he recognizes, that he can never quite catch up with, apologize to like he needs to.

And if you want to know how I know Belinda King put that little car there to try to close the circle, stop everything from happening, it's not that she told me, it's that, the morning Rob King beats Tommy Moore into the hospital, when Belinda King finally gets the call, she angles her head over, plucks her earrings out, and, just going by habit, starts to clink them into the marble ashtray by the phone, like always.

Except then she doesn't.

For the first time ever—Jonas checks, cleans it out himself—there's ashes in that ashtray, an empty pack of cigarettes hid up on top of the kitchen cabinets, and for years I fold this into my pocket, don't tell anybody, because it means Pete Manson really was there, like she said.

But he never was.

And he never told.

I will, though.

And Ms. Godfrey will read it at least, and know.

No.

Sheryl Ledbetter will read it.

You made it, she says to me back in the second chapter.

I don't know.

Minutes after she leaves me standing out there at the east corner of the new high school, the Diet Dr. Pepper can she was ashing in starts to blow away, so that I have to catch it, save it, can finally read that bronze plaque angled down by the three baby trees.

They're planted in honor of Mr. Brenhemin, Shop Teacher, 1928–2006.

He's still there at the corner of the school, watching the smoke rise.

We all are.

Growing Up Dead in Texas

Acknowledgments

Thanks to Janet Doggett, whose title this really is. Thanks to Darla Graham; if you hadn't posted an old photo of me online, I would never have even realized that I used to be somebody else. Thanks to my uncles, my aunt, to my mom, my dad, my brothers, my grandmother Ninee. To Gordon Highland, for saying a thing once about burying the lead; it made me wonder what a story that did that might be like. Thanks to all my art teachers, for never teaching me to draw. Thanks to Shooter Jennings; without tracks two through twelve, but especially twelve, I don't know how I could have done this. Thanks to *Monster-Quest*. Thanks to *Paradise Lost* (the documentary). *VALIS*. Duell McCall. Sam the Lion. Thanks to Brenda Mills and Mirka Hodurova and Christopher O'Riley and Jesse Wichterman, for reading early on. And Serena Chopra for reading first. And to Stefanie Hafey, for asking just how one goes about writing a novel for the first time. Thanks to those who remember when Challenger maybe really happened. Me too. Very distinctly. Thanks to Sidney Goldfarb, for saying once in a poem that this isn't true, but it's accurate. Thanks to Guy Intoci, for carrying this manuscript from coast to coast and then editing it until, like Mr. Seger says, it shines. Thanks to Kate Garrick, my agent through all of these books. And thanks finally and most sincerely to my wife Nancy, for everything, but apologies too; of most everybody who reads this, you're the one who'll have the hardest time, just because every one of these stories, you know some version of them. It won't fool you at all. But I never would.

Author Bio

STEPHEN GRAHAM JONES grew up in a land shaped by animals. The first bird he shot, he shot in a buffalo wallow. There would be countless more—owls and ducks, flying away with his pellet gun pellets lodged in them, doves he wouldn't learn to clean and eat for years, the blood on their yellow breasts like a dab of jelly on butter toast. Quail that were beautiful and pliant in his hand, scissortails that fell in looping arcs, their tails disappointing up close. Mounds of red and white and black woodpeckers his grandmother would point out for him, that, even with their bodies full of birdshot, still needed to be chased down in the tall grass. Once, on accident, a mockingbird that wanted to put him in jail, take away his gun. The hole he dug to hide it in was deep.

There would be more.

A bullbat, just to see if he could. A compact little hawk of a kind he's never seen again. He buried it in a hole he kicked in the dirt then took three steps away, found a pair of rattlesnakes mating, and watched them until they saw him and tried to break apart, couldn't. Hours later, skinless, headless, no guts, they still rose from the pan of grease he was cooking them in, struck at him with their blunt necks. Another time he walked onto a pair of sand rattlers, never knew how purple and pink their belly skin was until they were dead. That same year another rattlesnake pulled at his pantsleg but couldn't get through. He killed it for so long that the venom got in his arm, swelled it from wrist to elbow. Days after that, just to see if it was a thing he could do, or to see if it was something he shouldn't do, he got down on his knees with a ballpeen hammer, stared at a rattlesnake until it started striking.

He buried that snake in a deep hole with an owl he'd killed that same day, then, to keep them there, upended a fifty-five gallon drum, hammered it down around the owl and the snake until it was level with the ground, and told himself it was over, now—him, them. That he was sorry and it was over.

He was wrong.

Later that year he would stand in the brake lights of a pickup truck and help beat rabbits' heads against the bumper, because they weren't dead enough yet, then throw them into the pile already spilling over the bed rails. After that, with slide action rifles that felt so much like the air-pumps on his pellet guns, he would run down elk from the dancing beds of trucks, shoot prairie dogs to sight his gun in. Look through his scope one afternoon at what should have been a cow moose thirty yards out, broadside, but instead stood into a cinnamon grizzly, her two cubs tumbling into view.

That time, his great uncle guided the barrel of his gun down for him, and kept it there, and he looked over the top of his scope at that mother bear and wondered where his uncle had been three years ago in the buffalo wallow, when, out of birds but not daylight, he'd aimed for too long straight up, into a power line, and hit it, then felt the small slug immediately in the ground by his left foot, instead of the bones of his face. He dug the slug out. It was shaped like a mushroom, still hugging the power line, and he did any of a thousand things with it then. None of them right.

If I call it a novel, it is only because I don't know what else to call it...and, no doubt, as usual, I have exaggerated everything.
—MAUGHAM, CHABON